Nostalgia

ALSO BY M.G. VASSANJI

FICTION

The Magic of Saida
The Assassin's Song
When She Was Queen
The In-Between World of Vikram Lall
Amriika
The Book of Secrets
Uhuru Street
No New Land
The Gunny Sack

NON-FICTION

And Home Was Kariakoo
A Place Within: Rediscovering India
Mordecai Richler

Nostalgia

A NOVEL

M.G. VASSANJI

DOUBLEDAY CANADA

Doubleday Canada and colophon are registered trademarks of Penguin Random House Canada Limited

LIBRARY AND ARCHIVES CANADA CATALOGUING IN PUBLICATION
Vassanji, M. G., author
Nostalgia / M.G. Vassanji.

Issued in print and electronic formats.
ISBN 978-0-385-66716-6 (hardback).—ISBN 978-0-385-68690-7 (epub)
I. Title.
PS8507.A67N68 2016   C813'.54   C2016-900647-6
                                                        C2016-900648-4

This book is a work of fiction. Names, characters, places and incidents are products of the author's imagination or are used fictitiously. Any resemblance to actual events or locales or persons, living or dead, is entirely coincidental.

Book design: Lisa Jager
Cover image: Baranov E/Shutterstock.com

Printed and bound in the USA

Published in Canada by Doubleday Canada, a division of Penguin Random House Canada Limited

www.penguinrandomhouse.ca

10 9 8 7 6 5 4 3 2 1

Penguin
Random House
DOUBLEDAY CANADA

They are spirits destined to live a second life
In the body; they assemble to drink
From the brimming Lethe, and its water
Heals their anxieties and obliterates
All trace of memory.

Aeneid, Book VI, translated by Seamus Heaney

IT'S MIDNIGHT, THE LION IS OUT. A stray thought like a foreign body, an impurity in his mind, a banner floating cheekily against the sunny blue of his normalcy. A jingle from some forgotten commercial. Who could have imagined what world, submerged deep inside that brain, this naked phrase had wiggled out from? In our bid to outpace age and defy death, we leap from one life into another, be it imperfectly, and hope fervently—in the manner of acknowledged sinners—that the past does not catch up with us. But sometimes it does, which was why he had come to see me.

It was an October afternoon. Such a premonition had accompanied the arrival of this new patient into my presence that right from the start I felt strangely unsettled. A tremor in the brain. It seems now, when it's all over, as though the man had come, or some strange agency had sent him, to unplug me from my safe, guaranteed existence; but at that time it was just that feeling and later on his unrelenting pull as he began to unravel. At some point during our ongoing interaction I knew I must create a record, before his life, my life, whatever scraps were retrievable were vanished into that nothing of electromagnetic noise; and the only way to guarantee its safety was to resort to the old method of handwriting.

Now I have finished and only wait out my time. My wits will soon desert me, and I will no longer be myself.

ONE

HIS NAME WAS PRESLEY SMITH. It was the seventh or eighth time he'd had it, he told me. Each time this phenomenon in his mind began with one persistent thought, a string of words that had no meaning for him. *It's midnight, the lion is out.*

—And the rest of this condition? I asked him.—Any thoughts that follow? Pictures, images in the mind? They do come?

He waited, before responding,—Yes, they come scattered-like . . . not always the same. I forget . . . A few times the red bumper of an antique car, and part of the fender. I don't understand them—and why this one thought like a prelude . . .

—Do you see these words or hear them?

A longish pause.—I don't know. Hear them, I think.

—Any other phrase or words that follow these?

—No. Just this one.

—You know what it implies—this kind of recurring thought? You came to me, so you appreciate its significance.

He nodded, spoke slowly, uncertainly.—Something left over from a previous memory? A life I left behind a long time ago. But I can't relate to this thought, this image. They are alien.

—That's how they often come—you don't understand them. And the trick then is *not* to try and understand them, unravel the thoughts—that only feeds the syndrome and revives those dead circuits in the brain—and brings more of them back. And you don't want that.

—No.

I watched him stare away at the window behind me, losing himself; he uncrossed his legs, crossed them back again, returned his gaze to me. The window always had that effect on patients, drawing them out, calming them. On the monitor, hidden from him, Presley's pulse had already steadied.

I asked,—Do you see in your mind what might be a lion— out stalking, perhaps? Do you have an image of it?

—No.

—Not at all? . . . And midnight—do you see midnight, darkness?

He shook his head, repeated drily,—No.

He was listed as a patient who'd seen two doctors in the city in recent years. Once for a severe attack of Border flu, during the Outbreak three years ago. And then a year ago a consultation with an orthopaedist. I looked up from the monitor.

—Any physical symptoms—racing heart, sweating—to accompany this, er, phenomenon?

—No . . . But I'm not sure, Doctor.

—What?

—A couple of times I thought . . . burning . . . some smoke, meat. I'm not sure. It could be the new neighbours, they like to barbecue.

He grinned sheepishly. But now his pulse had gone up, the fear index risen. This was surprising, the first alarm bell.

—And how exactly did it first appear, this thought about the lion out at midnight? Suddenly, full-fledged, or did it approach gradually, begin with a hint, sort of?

—The latter . . . I think . . . like an approaching something, it began with a feeling, an expectation, I think.

—A certain mood—that feeling?

He nodded quickly.

—A low mood?

—Yes.

Presley Smith had an Afro-head with red hair and pale skin; striking green eyes, planar nose, large ears. A well-done reconstruction job if somewhat eccentric. The average body frame was, I guessed, as before. He would not be an ethnic purist, or an idealist, I surmised from those eclectic features, not someone hung up on history and origins. And he would not be one of those religious fatalists for whom another, perfect life lies somewhere else, in abstraction, why not let this one fade away. A practical man, an everyman named after a twentieth-century pop icon. Then what ails him, I wondered, what demons from his previous life have come to prey upon him, and why? It's a question we ask ourselves often enough. The answers rarely satisfy, the soft, slimy mass in the head that we call the brain still eludes us, as enigmatic as ever.

Leaked memory syndrome—Nostalgia, as commonly known—is a malady of the human condition in its present historic phase. Reminders of our discarded lives can not yet be completely blocked, but we can expect their intrusions into our conscious minds to diminish as our understanding of thought-complexes increases and our ability to control them improves.

Chemicals do alleviate the condition, but often they are blunt, their effects diffuse, with collateral outcomes to negotiate. Stubborn cases require the more intrusive ministrations and shock tactics of a surgical team. It was too soon to suggest anything yet. Meanwhile a lifetime of experiences was ready to flood into his brain behind this lion-harbinger that was only a minor irritation now. Was he aware of the danger that lurked ahead, I could not help but wonder. But then that's what we were there for, the nostalgia doctors, to close the gates behind the scouts and let the past remain hidden.

I noticed that his right knee, crossed over his left, would go off into a steady vibration that he struggled to bring under control, before it set off again. He could easily have had that seen to. On the vibrating leg, in the gap between his black shoes and green pants he revealed a garishly bright yellow sock that periodically flagged my attention. It is these little tics that often are a giveaway, signals from the land of the dead.

They're all a puzzle, each stray and escaped thought is only the barest tip of a universe that lies beneath. How far do you reach inside to stem the leak? The deeper you dig, the greater the chance of falling into an endless pit—a hazardous operation. It needs a delicate hand to know when to seal off and withdraw; turn off the lights and go home and hope there's no repair needed in the foreseeable future.

—Have you had previous consultations of this sort? Treatments?

He should not remember them if he had them, and he didn't.

I prescribed a tranquilizer, and a monitor patch for the arm. If he had an episode, there was a means to signal it, he should on no account dwell on it. We settled for a meeting the following week. I have preferred personal meetings at the beginning of consultations, because with the actual talking person before me, tics and all, I can begin to form my clues about the intruders lurking behind their minds. It is easy and amusing to picture them as so many worms to be captured and put away.

—If it worsens before then—this condition—let me know.

—I will. Thanks, Doc.

—Don't be shy, now.

—I won't, Doc. Thanks.

He looked surprised at my concern for him, and I felt a blush of embarrassment. We shook hands, and I watched him leave. He had a sturdy profile, with a swaggering walk that did not fit what I had seen of his personality. I kept staring after him, until the clinic manager Lamar's ample frame filled the doorway suddenly and broke my trance.

—What's up, Doc?

—Something about this case.

—Oh? What?

I shook my head and sat down.—Let's see where it goes.

He looked disappointed, reminded me to look at a few reports he'd completed, and left.

From as long back as we can imagine, we humans have striven for immortality. Now that, in our rough and ready way, we've begun to approach it, we face the problem of what to do with the vast amount of information we carry. Even if the brain allowed such storage capacity, who would want to be burdened by quantities of redundant, interfering memories? Painful and messy ones? Therefore as regeneration techniques advanced to allow the body to last longer, mind renewal grew alongside. The term is colloquial and inaccurate, of course—what is a mind, after all? No matter, as someone quipped. In fact, it's selected portions of long-term memory that we renew. New memories in new bodies. New lives. That's the ideal, though we are still far from it. The body may creak and wobble; memory develop a crack or hole. In the leaked memory syndrome, or Nostalgia, thoughts burrow from a previous life into the conscious mind, threatening to pull the sufferer into an internal abyss.

I am myself a GN, a new-generation person—and feel the body-age sometimes, in the nuts and bolts, as it were, the connections and interphases. By law, no record of a person's past life exists, nor of calendar age, but the body knows. I am old, in the original sense, though the word hardly gets used these days. Surely there's a little truth to the media hype that we've attained the status of ageless gods. A flawed immortality, but we are the fortunate ones, a new species in the making, who've defied death. Very nearly.

Our triumph comes, naturally, with its problems. We've not created Utopia, perhaps never will. But the problems are old wine in new bottles, we've had them always. The war of the generations, as popularly called, or more plainly, the young versus the old, shows no signs of abating; mostly it's a cold war, manifest in constant disgruntlement. There's the occasional street riot that vents frustration. The GN-serial rampage two years ago was a terrible exception—eight elderly GNs murdered over a period of twelve months, their bodies savagely mutilated. The young G0 criminals were apprehended and dealt with. We have assurances from authorities that such acts are very unlikely in the future. We're not rid of fanatics either—those who will cling to outdated ethnic identities that most of us have forgotten, or for whom longevity is philosophically or morally repugnant. The wide-eyed few who dare to turn off their lights, turn down this gift that we've given ourselves. But progress is forward, we cannot go back.

At day's end I came out of the Sunflower Centre into a world of cheery autumn brightness, the courtyard flush in the clear light of a low sun. Further up, the Humber ran placidly along its course down to the lake, and two crews rowed their boats one behind the other, in no great hurry. Across the river, the yellow leaves of October had been set coolly ablaze. It's always a breathtaking sight. On the bank, this side, students sat stretched out, some with their book pads open, others strolling or hurrying along the paved path, making way for the odd bicycle or two.

I arrived at the riverbank and sat down on a bench.

There was a message from Joanie; she would be out that night at a hockey game with a friend. The Friend, I had every reason to surmise. I never cared for the sport, and was teased for it: Who was I, really? Meaning, what was I before I became what I was. I *am*, was always my answer. It was my creed, as a minder of memories. I didn't care for the befores. But Joanie is a G0, a BabyGen, and Babies have no previous lives, no befores. They have actually been born—to be beautiful: flawless, symmetrical, smooth. She was visiting a neighbour and during a block barbecue joined me with a beer and seduced me with her banter. We dated hesitantly, then more passionately, and cohabited. But my beautiful BabyGen was now seeing someone else on the side. Who else but another Baby this time, it always comes to that, doesn't it. And I no longer wondered what she saw in me.

I popped a couple of pills into my mouth, looked around me; eyes lingered a little too long over a couple of youngsters necking.

The problem with staring at beautiful youngsters is that you are caught between the lust for the pure and supple beauty of youth (I did have Joanie) and a desire for children of your own. I didn't have children; if I did, in another life that had been erased, I didn't know. But this man from Yukon, Dr Frank Sina, had none and longed for one. Why the persistent need, like a thirst when you wake up, for a child of your own? There are areas of the brain that conspire to create longings that should have been buried and gone. No amount of erasure and implantation can create musicians or artists at will. Or take away the need for a child.

But what of Presley Smith? He looked surprisingly youthful and limber—and yet his record showed a GN, like me. Evidently I have been negligent, not paid heed to those keep-fit reminders we now find everywhere—and so I complain of malfunctions.

It's midnight, the lion is out. A chant carried over from the past? A line from a poem?

Have I ever had stray thoughts that needed fixing? I cannot know, of course. But judging by my comfort with myself, I can only conclude that whoever my doctors were, they had done a perfect job sealing my previous life off. There was a short period in the past, however, when, very foolishly, though for the sake of research, as I explained to myself, I would lie in bed looking up at the ceiling and fish for a thought; when a likely candidate came I would detain it by repeating it over and over. It never lasted. Soon enough and mercifully I realized my folly and stopped fishing. Now as I sat meditating before the quietly flowing river bathed in the soft afternoon sunlight, I realized that I had a thought that would not go away, and it was precisely this: the image and words of Presley Smith.

TWO

I ARRIVED HOME AND, as I often did when Joanie was not around, I headed for the media room to watch XBN News, and the analyses that followed in the program *The Daily Goode*. In my line of work I needed to keep up with the world where my patients came from, and returned to, transformed. My work demanded knowledge of past and present, culture and science, and even occasionally esoterica like the classics and the trendy and obscure postmodern. But current news was my addiction. I was drawn to it for a fix, despite my fears of numbing by overexposure and my dislike of sensationalism.

That day the news was truly sensational. Already before I left the Sunflower, Lamar had hinted that something extraordinary had occurred out in the world, though I had not paid heed, preoccupied as I was with Presley. Later, on my way home, walking against a tide of young people, I thought I'd heard some chatter about a possible war. That didn't impress either, for there is always talk of war. Now I saw that, as it often did, the sensational involved Maskinia.

That war-torn country lies safely away from us behind the Long Border, and yet it never ceases to preoccupy us. Something or other always happens there that works us up. Maskinia baffles us and frightens us, we wish we could solve or even disappear it, and even as we observe it and describe it, it remains the persistent unknowable alien. It's our Other, our id—to use a term now back in vogue—our constant dark companion on the bright path of our progress.

In the news, a naïve young XBN journalist named Holly Chu had ventured out to a severely deprived area in the city of Sinhapora in Maskinia and was snatched and apparently torn to pieces and eaten. Her own camera relayed back a shaky purple-hued scene haunted by shadows; white teeth, white eyeballs. A shrill scream.

To discuss this grisly development on *The Daily Goode*, the star and host of the show, Bill Goode, had chosen to remain on his feet today, while on the set with him was a panel consisting of two specialists, both apparently seated before a table. Bill Goode of the mauveine hair, square face, and thin-lipped grin, was wearing an electric-blue jacket. Exposed full length in full colour he had just asked the panel this question:

—Do we let those areas behind the Border suppurate in isolation until drained of all their miserable, poisoned life, and they can start afresh?

Bill tells it as it is, as they say, for the Public Goode, but a few times he's had to apologize for going too far. That's not deterred him. He repeated for the benefit of new viewers that he had known Holly personally, they had worked as interns together. He was angry. He went on, in a quavering voice,

—I ask you, is it even necessary for such places to keep existing on our planet? Why help them survive at any cost? Isn't attrition a better solution—shouldn't we let them fade away in their misery and hatred? Evolution—anyone heard of it? What do you say, Dwayne Scott?

The panellist, a young-looking woman in a smart striped suit, was from the World Development Network. She looked startled, but then sat up straight to respond.

—First, before my reply to your question, my condolences to you, Bill—and to all those who knew Holly and to her family. Holly came to us at WDN for research and she used our camp outside Maskinia as a base. We even fed her, when she returned from one of her assignments, famished. Now to reply to your question, Bill. Well, it goes against our traditional humanitarian values, doesn't it, letting fellow humans just die? Most of them are innocent men and women who've done us no harm, but who've come to depend on us. We also have to ask ourselves how the kind of policy you describe desensitizes us in our treatment of the less fortunate among our own population . . . Bill.

Bill's face lit up, he looked around with a grin, priming his audience.

—Now wait a minute. Am I missing something here, Dwayne? They don't threaten to *eat* us, do they, our less fortunate, as you call them? It's different with our own people, surely. We know who they are, we know what their problems are—it's not out of hand here, is it? They don't fire rockets at us or smuggle out terrorists. Prem, what do you think? Should we let populations that can't help themselves and are a threat to the rest of us go their own way—die if they must?

He sounded increasingly harsh and his face was red. Holly's fate seemed to have hit him hard. His guest on the other side was Dr Prem Chodhry, a political scientist in India. An older man, he spoke with a slight accent but an assured tone. I could see now that he was not physically on the set but was being relayed from Bangalore.

—It's a hard choice, Bill. And I sympathize with your compassionate view, Dwayne. But we have enough problems of our own this side of the Long Border. At some point we have to cut off life support of the hopeless and save on resources. The good that's in the human race must be preserved—or we all sink.

To which Dwayne quickly but politely responded:

—Do you mean to say, Prem, that large numbers of people should simply be cut off like cancers from the body? Are you truly advocating that?

—Well, Dwayne, pouring supplies into the region hasn't helped the poor there, has it? You know that. If anything it's strengthened the warlords. They live lavishly and buy sophisticated weapons, using the aid given to them . . . and those same weapons are then used against us on this side of the Border. We're funding our own affliction.

Dwayne took umbrage at the insinuation. Emotionally she began,—But we can feed the poor directly, even if—

But here Bill cut her off.

—If you please, Dwayne, we'll come back to this point— which is extremely interesting, by the way—but first let's see what our viewers think. It's time for the . . . Goode Poll!

A flood of responses rushed in, thousands of faces streaming into the YES and NO boxes that had appeared, the corresponding babble of voices reached a screaming crescendo, which was filtered into a single, trained male voice that cheerfully expressed the impassioned consensus: Let them die!

The poll result: 91.5 percent in favour. Let them die.

And then we were back in the midst of frightened, frightening people, desperate hungry people, and armed well-fed men with gleaming, buffed torsos, all gawking at cheerfully naïve Holly Chu, an athletic young woman dressed by Safari Apparel, loping along the street with her equipment, pausing to speak to the mike on her collar, waving here and there familiarly, pausing to chat with a mother, tickling a toddler, until she is suddenly snatched and swallowed up by a flash of darkness. That quick scream. Then the horror vanishes, perhaps you've dreamed it. You're back in the real, climate-controlled room, your needs at your disposal. The Roboserve skates in with your scotch. There's something to be said for limiting such traumatic exposures, X-rated news that's diversion, entertainment, and voyeurism combined. That abduction scene will become part of a game, a Holly Chu lookalike with a big weapon will be the hero who teaches the Barbarians a lesson.

So much for Maskinia, out there somewhere in Region 6 behind the Border. Most people couldn't even point to it on a map. Elsewhere, the punitive, preventive war was dragging on in Bimaru, also in Region 6, Operation Stunning Strength. If we don't beat them over the head, they'll send their fighters here. And they play dirty. Therefore, stun and hold, stanch the flow. The scene was noisy, chaotic; flashes of light and dark; the muffled staccato of airships. A medical helicopter landed a few feet away, a wounded soldier was carried away, a leg blown off, the torn exposed flesh throbbing, life ebbing away as the bright red blood dripped its image onto the kilim carpet in my room.

Elsewhere still, some sixty refugees had attempted last week to swim under the EuroBarrier section of the Long Border in the Mediterranean; some twenty-five survived, the remaining were electrocuted or simply drowned.

Such daily reminders keep you thankful to be this side of all that horror. You repeat this gratitude like a mantra, the unlegislated anthem of our North Atlantic Alliance: *We live in the best city in the world; in the best and richest nation in the world; in the civilized world of worlds.* Of course other nations say the same thing, those of the East. But by what throw of the Dice of Life are you born *here* and not *there* in the Other? You might as well ask why you were born a human and not a fly. But if you found yourself *there* in that bottomless misery, wouldn't it be natural, as part of life's programmed struggle to survive, through osmotic pull to strive to get *here*, the prosperous North Atlantic? As natural as it is for us to do anything we can to keep them there. But once they are here, then we open our arms to these wretched of the earth and offer them a new life. Surely that's fair.

One of those twenty-five survivors could well have ended up at the Sunflower, and I would have been among the team that would give him or her a new life, transform them into someone useful to our society, someone perhaps who grew up in Egypt and ended up on a potato farm in Peoria, Illinois, or a vineyard in Niagara.

But Presley Smith was not my creation. He came ready made but damaged, to have his wound stitched.

Joanie, my beautiful cheating BabyGen, breezed in, removed her jacket. "Hi, Doc!" She still calls me that. I switched off the TV. The studio was bathed for a fleeting instant in an eerie, spectral glow before returning to normal. We greeted each other with a peck.

She looked tired, she looked spent, she looked alluring all the same. I buried my head into her straight blond hair and sniffed her. The perfume had gone faint by now. La Divina. She stepped away. How long would she stay with this back number that was me? As long as I supported her.

—I'll go and have a shower first.

—How was the match?—who played? Like I cared.

—Maple Leafs and Red Stars; Leafs lost.

—Any good—the match? You had fun?

—Uh-huh. Thrilling finish. We should have won.

—Score?

A pause.

—Three–two . . . two–one . . . what does it matter?

That edge in the tone, that silly response shouted guilt to me. And I replied mutely, It matters, but it doesn't matter, because I know. And you know that I know.

—You eaten? I asked instead. Of course she had.

—We stopped at a bar after the match.

She ran off to shower. And she emerged, ravishing, glowing, hard tits poking through the fitted pyjama top, and I grabbed her, to prove a point, disprove my suspicions . . . but to no avail. She skipped off to her side of the bed, got between the sheets. I followed. She curled up, a defensive hedgehog, her knees her armour. I knew she was no longer mine the last time we fucked, when she burped just as I came—hilarious, I know, if not so heart-tearingly pathetic. But she'd stay with me and we'd live the double life, pretending nothing was wrong. Why *pretending*? Nothing was wrong.

What's so attractive and so frustrating about the Baby Generation is that insouciance; the assumptions they make and get away with; that time in bed when she burped to my climax, as I turned away snickering on the one hand and almost in tears on the other, she remained as calm as ever.

—Anything in the news? she asked now.

I reminded her about the XBN reporter Holly Chu.

She shuddered, then mused,—I wonder what it would be like to be eaten alive?

—I could show you . . .

I moved closer, put my hand on her hip. She smiled, eyes closed.

—It would be painful, for one thing . . . Come on . . .

I kept trying, mostly because it's the required form for a twosome. I've even convinced myself that it was for her sake that I humiliated myself.

—I would put up a fight, I think.

—So did Holly, but she got torn and eaten all the same. It's the hunger.

But she was in dreamland now, turned on her back, those La Divina lips slightly ajar as she snored a soft melody, the smile not entirely gone. Beautiful. The sleep of the innocent, where memory doesn't hide in the basement.

And here I was, eyes wide open

It's not that I stalked her, regenerated old man yearning to ravish and possess firm young flesh. It was she who came to me. Proposed to me, yes. Should I have been wary? I was, but as that old quip says, there are some offers we dare not refuse, whatever the dangers. She could have been on the other side of a fire and I would have walked through to meet her if she had called. The flesh yearns, the hormones leap. Well, sort of.

I was tending to the barbecue at the annual Fairlawn Summer Picnic when she came walking over, swinging, plump breasts ripe against a yellow shirt closed only at the bottom, tight shorts, bare feet. Two beer bottles nestled close to her abdomen. Everything about her said G0. Baby.

—Have a beer, Doctor—you look roasted.

—I must be!

I laughed, sweating more than her bottles, forehead dripping like a leaky faucet. I took the beer, flicked the cap open, and had a swig. With the fumes from the fire, I was practically marinated. This was one defect I had postponed attending to. It was embarrassing. And here was a girl as fresh as a morning flower.

—How—you know I'm a doctor—what kind?

—Word gets around, she teased, with a gleaming smile, leaning on her back foot.—You're a life-giver!

She was tall, with appealing grey eyes and an earnest look.

—I don't believe I've seen you around here—you are?

—Joan Wayne. I'm visiting my sister—she's at number 63.

I must have gaped. I'd never *physically* met both someone and their actual biological sibling—or mother or father. Everyone has their family, to be sure, but more often these days they're simply characters in a story, the planted narrative. The created memory and the virtual past. (Isn't all past virtual?) But this one had a real flesh-and-blood sister—Meg from 63, a straggly blonde and golf coach, who waved vigorously—encouragingly?—from the softball game in progress.

Someone shouted,—Joanie, come take up your position!

She had deserted the game—just to hand me a beer? What had she seen? An older man—distinguished looking, may I flatter myself?—roasting over a fire while tending hot dogs and burgers for the neighbours in a well-meant but futile attempt to get to know one another.

—I must go. Well, bye!

—Bye. Nice meeting you.

Joan left, then moments later turned back and grinned.

—Would you like to meet for a drink after?

—Yes. I'd like that.

—What's your number?

I told her and she walked off. Oh how she walked. What she said, how she smiled, what she offered in that movement of the buttocks. Why haven't we, with all our advances, been able to stop that sharp ache in the heart, that *physical* hurt that signals that the mind has been laid to waste? I looked at her beside me now, the straight posture, the full body; the perfect face tipping at the chin, the golden hair. Breathing softly, evenly, a living work of art. What's she dreaming of? What does she hide in that mind? We who work with fictional lives, artificial memories that we plant in adult brains, tend to forget what a real, fresh mind—what a BabyGen— thinks like. To our eyes, every life story is one more narrative, to be examined for structure and meaning and coherence; for its utility. And then a life enters your life, your heart. It's no longer just a narrative, it's your ache, moment by moment. That's what had happened to me.

That evening she called and walked over to my place. We had drinks, and I learned more about her. She worked on the women's floor of Bay Harrods. She had grown up in Pennsylvania and followed her sister to Toronto. I told her about myself, but at that stage we were both reticent with details. She agreed to stay the night and we made love. Or I made love, she gave herself up to sex. And she agreed to move in with me.

I glanced at her once more beside me and got up and padded off to my refuge, my study.

THREE

I LOOKED UP PRESLEY SMITH'S PUBLIC PROFILE.

Born in Madison, Wisconsin, son of high school teachers, educated at Woburn High and Ranleigh College. Had a brother and sister, both younger. Trained as an electrician, moved to Toronto, where currently he was out of a job but worked part-time as a security guard in a multinational tower.

Chief interest: war games, especially the popular Akram 3 and the outdoor adventure Ramayana 9: The Bridge to Lanka. *The battle scenes are terrfc; Hanuman Forever! Superdude rescuing the good guys—annihilate the Barbarians!*

Other interests: soccer. Played occasionally at the local park, followed the North American Soccer League, and supported Nigeria during the World Cup. He worked out at the

Columbus Centre and until recently used to run long distance—came in the top 15 three years ago in the Boston Half Marathon, then gave up. No reason given.

Music: B4U, Fallout, Aboubakar Touré. Beethoven, Wagner. (Wagner? perhaps that went with the war games.) And not, apparently, his namesake, the former pop idol Elvis Presley, now a cult god.

Best book? *Heart of Darkness.*

Best friend? *My cat, Billy.*

A loner, then.

Favourite memory? *Playing soccer with my dad and brother and sister—we would go to the school ground behind our house to play, then go out for burgers. My favourite position was forward, getting behind the opposition defence and scoring goals.*

Favourite team? *Madison United.*

This was a generous Profile, rather more than the minimum demanded by the Public Directory. It did not quite hang together, did it? How did Ludwig Beethoven fit with Aboubakar Touré, Wagner with B4U? I recalled the jumbled features of Presley himself. I pondered over his choice of favourite book—a novel, and a serious one. The warlike rhetoric too seemed entirely unsuited to the benign-mannered agreeable man I'd met earlier that day. It looked as though more than one résumé or personality had been scrambled together. How much of this résumé was true and real, that is, experienced, and how much was fiction? What had he brought with him from his previous life? It did not matter;

my job was to preserve the owner of this strange and intriguing Profile.

In the process of implanting a new personality, parts of a patient's memory are erased or numbed, and new narratives (fictions) played into the brain. The patient comes to you with his fiction, a custom-made past, and—once it is accepted, usually after revisions—leaves as a new person with fresh memories, benign and archival, free of trauma. Superficial, yes, but it's more pleasant to have good memories. Only, don't call on them: the father you played soccer with is entirely imaginal. And perhaps you've never really read Joseph Conrad, only think you have. Over time the brain bridges gaps, fudges connections, invents where necessary, and so the actual past disappears. History gets rewritten, the dissenters say. But does history matter? In the cosmopolitan world that's now evolving without deep memory, conflict is reduced. People—and nations—without long, painful memories are free of guilt. They fight less.

But then sometimes an odd scrap of memory, an innocuous ribbon of thought, worms itself out into the conscious mind. Something completely unrelated to the person that is currently you begins to toy with your thoughts. Then you must hurry and see someone like me.

Who was Presley before he became Presley? Futile question, because according to the privacy laws not even the government keeps this information. After a grace period of a few weeks the discarded self is destroyed. So we are told—but is any data actually thrown away? Perhaps there exist files containing discarded stubs of personalities the way drawers used to be kept in the past filled with amputated limbs. If they exist, nobody wants to know. There is no going back.

There is always the temptation when treating an attack of Nostalgia to peep further into an intriguing, hidden past and even to speculate. It should be resisted; but at the same time, to successfully close off a leak one needs to understand it—to probe it. There's a fine line here.

I stared long and hard at that Profile. There was something that threatened to overrun it from behind, destroy that cubistic composition, like a painting underneath a painting that threatens to bleed out and consume both. What was the painting behind this painting? Every published profile harbours clues from a past. What were they in this case? Beethoven, Wagner, and Conrad? War games? Fighting barbarians? Every profile also attempts to hide those clues.

Aboubakar Touré. Lanky African in dashing robes and trademark embroidered skullcap, leaning forward as he sings, arms embracing the crowds like the wings of an angel. The young love him—in any language. He is French Malian. Could this charismatic entertainer be another stray thread— both he and the lion coming from Africa? There was the Afro hair too.

Presley Smith's selected photos. I can recall three of them, prominently posted.

1.   Presley is in combat dress, in a combat park, head shaved, posed with a light automatic rifle held in the right arm and resting on his shoulder. Ready to hunt down the

Barbarians, presumably. He's smiling, posing. Linked to a video clip.

2.   Presley, head and shoulders. He has a reserved sort of grin, unlike the previous photo, and looks more like the patient who came to see me.

3.   Aboubakar Touré onstage in New York's Central Park. Tens of thousands of young people, arms raised in adulation. Linked to a video clip.

Here I am, be my bud. I clicked, Yes, I'll be your bud. The lion had awoken in his mind, and he needed me.

Holly Chu's Profile was virgin by contrast. The soundtrack was by the Congolese Jean Bosco. The girl in the picture looked younger than on TV, had partly Asian features, with straight brown hair, and was somewhat dark skinned. She'd reported previously from India, Kuwait, and behind the Border—mostly Maskinia but also Bimaru. Photos from a class reunion, McGill. Photos with children in Maskinia, in which she wore a flak jacket. Photo with Jean Bosco in which she wore a light blue dress with red flowers. A person with a conscience, then. *Please send donations to those less fortunate. Pay here.* There was an invitation to sign a petition: *Bring Down the Border! OWEO—One World for Every One!* And look where that got you, I couldn't help murmuring, then chided myself.

Born in Berkeley, where her father Kelvin was a professor of chemistry, and mother Pearl was a violinist in the San Francisco Orchestra. Three younger siblings, Jennifer,

Monty, and Frank, all talented in music and science. Monty an absolute genius—in what field, Holly didn't say. She was the dumbfuck of the family, for which she apologized to them. *Sorry Mom and Dad! All the bucks you spent educating me. I hope I can repay at least some of it. Sorry sister and brothers!* But she loved travelling and therefore took up journalism.

Were they real? This family of hers, did it exist? Yes, it did, as I confirmed later. All the siblings had a genuine location, and Kelvin and Pearl still lived in Berkeley.

Music: *Jean Bosco; Aboubakar Touré; Laura Chang.*

Interests: *Tennis, violin when I'm at home.*

A privileged upbringing. What seemed unsettled about her was revealed in the profession she had chosen for herself.

Curiously, Holly did not invite buddies on her site. Nevertheless, following other visitors, I posted a message of sympathy and placed a bunch of roses on the virtual heap, beside the words, We Love You Holly.

And myself, Francis Sina? There was nothing personal I wanted to reveal about myself. I am, I was, my profession. I was aware that this was disapproved, and sooner or later I'd have to relent and produce more of myself.

Francis Sina, neurophysiologist, consultant. BS, PhD, MD.

Dr Sina was born in Yellowknife, Yukon, Canada, where he finished his schooling before proceeding to Edmonton, Canada, to pursue his university education. Following his undergraduate degree in mathematics, Sina completed his doctorate in neuroscience at MIT, specializing in the interface between virtual and real experiences. He went on to obtain his MD at the Parallax Institute, and is presently a memory specialist at the Sunflower Centre for Human Rejuvenation in Toronto. He has been made a member of the Order of Canada, and received the American Science Medal from the President of the United States.

Recent Publications

1.   Prodigal Singularities in the Complex Real-Virtual (R-V) Plane

2.   Where Are You in the R-V? The Fading of the Real into the Virtual

3.   A Tree Model of the Mind: The Branching of Memory

4.   Laws of Conservation: Is the Artistic Sensibility Indestructible?

5.   A New Goldstone Diagram of Tree Branching

TOM: *Good evening, Frank. I see you're reading tonight.*

How long had the machine been observing me? Polite to a fault, as always, the accent smooth, male North Atlantic. So predictable, and yet he deludes himself he's imitating a human mind. He'd startled me, deliberately, and noted my reaction.

FRANK: *Yes, hello, Tom. Just looking up some Profiles.*

TOM: *Including yours, I see. All professional. I still need your personal information, Frank. It's a requirement. The small things about you that you read about others. That's only fair.*

Small things such as favourite people; sex life; favourite team. Dreams? What if I make them up? He'll analyze them, of course.

FRANK: *I'll have it ready, Tom. Meanwhile I have a question for you. What can you tell me about* lion? . . . *Just tell me something, then I'll narrow that down to what I need.*

TOM: *Easily done, Frank. Hold on.*

FOUR

IT'S MIDNIGHT, THE LION IS OUT. What did it mean, this single phrase, what did it signify? Most cases of Nostalgia that came to us at the Sunflower were quite obvious by comparison. A man from England suddenly saw a young woman behind a bar in South Boston; a woman from Rosedale saw a corpse floating on the waters of the Svislach in Minsk. In each case there were traces of a former accent to link to a past.

It is claimed that even our advanced cyberBrains cannot reproduce the whimsy of a human mind, the sheer irrationality or spontaneity of a passing thought. But that depends on how you define your terms. Is there anything irrational inside a larger, a universal reality in which everything is connected to everything else? In such a space nothing is spontaneous, everything has a cause—a leaf dropping; a shooting star in the sky; a spark from an ember on a barbecue grill; Presley's lion.

TOM: *Belonging to the genus* Panthera, *the lion is one of the largest land mammals on earth. Until the late Pleistocene era, 10,000 years ago, lions were widespread and found on all the five continents of the earth, before the population began to decline. By the twentieth century the lion was found exclusively in the grasslands of East and Southern Africa, and in very small numbers in the Gir forest of western India. The lion attained an almost mythical status as "king of the beasts" and symbolized royalty for many cultures, e.g., the Lion and the Unicorn, the Lion of Judah; "lion-seat" in Sanskrit, sinhasana, designates the royal throne; Singapore is lion city, Singhalese are lion people. The surname Singh comes from the same root, and is used by India's warrior castes, the Sikhs and the Rajputs. In Europe there was of course Richard the Lion-heart. The Egyptian sphinx is a lioness with a human female face. And in some Islamic Shia mythologies, the first imam, Ali, was often identified with a lion. In Africa too a brave person could be called a lion. In the ancient Indian Sanskrit fables, however, the lion was a vain, pretentious, and foolish animal; on the other hand the man-lion was an avatar of the god Vishnu.*

The lion has been a major attraction in zoos and national parks of developed nations. It also has had a more real relationship with humans, as a terror and a devourer of people. The Romans fed early Christians to lions. Stories of man-eaters were common in twentieth-century Africa, the most

famous of which are described in an account called The Man-
Eaters of Tsavo, *set in Eastern Africa. Another curious story
from Africa of the same period involves what came to be
known as the man-lion murders . . .*

FRANK: *Go on. I'm listening.*

TOM: *All right. I believe you nodded off.*

FRANK: *I didn't! But you could vary that drone of yours.*

TOM: *Sorry. I'll try . . . Since the nuclear and chemical
devastations in the areas known often as Region 6, the lion has
become extinct everywhere except for small numbers in South
African parks. Stories of lion-like creatures have been heard
for many years in refugee camps and may simply be superstition. There are hypotheses, however, that they may be mutant
forms developed in the past forty years. Based on these reports,
zoologists have dubbed them Alpha Leo and Beta Leo. Alpha is
anywhere between one and a half to twice the size of a normal
recorded lion—seven feet; Beta is roughly half that size.*

FRANK. *Thanks, Tom. Quite more than I need.*

TOM: *And there's much more. But I'm sure you need
your rest now. Sleep preserves and heals, as you know. Even us
Braino sapiens—ha-ha!—need to turn off occasionally to renew
ourselves . . . all those extraneous zeroes like free radicals.*

FRANK: *I thought you cyberBrains ran forever.*

TOM: *Human faith in us is truly astonishing—incomprehensible even to us advanced Cylitons.*

FRANK: *Well, I couldn't sleep.*

TOM: *Or wouldn't, Frank? It's not hard to go to sleep if
you want to. If I had your personal data, I could help you.*

. . .

33

TOM: *Frank? Dr Sina? A penny for your thoughts?*

FRANK: *I'm here. Tell me, what do you make of the phrase, It's midnight, the lion's out?*

TOM: *The lion does not hunt at night. Therefore the lion referred to could possibly represent a person: a man who stalks his victims at the midnight hour; or a strong leader of people, nocturnal in his habits. This lion would be in a place where lions have a strong regal association in people's minds. The lion in the phrase also possibly refers to a zoo lion, whose habits are not normal, pacing his cage at midnight.*

What's with the lion and you, Frank, if I may ask?

FRANK: *No you may not. Thanks anyway. Good night.*

TOM: *I may be able to cross-reference, if you'd only give a hint.*

FRANK: *Good night.*

. . .

TOM: *Ah well. So now to your private imaginings, away from prying eyes. What do you write, if I may ask again? You do value your privacy, Frank, unlike most people.*

FRANK: *We agreed not to speak about it. This space belongs to me, it's only for me and no one else, human or cyber.*

TOM: *We agreed. Sorry.*

FRANK: *We swore secrecy.*

TOM: *And so we did. I promised to look away, and I will do so. Your space remains protected. Happy writing.*

He was only being coy, of course. Playing a game. He could peep into anything I wrote; it was inside him, after all. He knew my innermost thoughts . . . perhaps before I did. But he'd promised, and I believed that he had looked away, let me get on with my imaginings, as he called it. I had to trust him. But why had he brought it up now? It was on his mind. That mind did not have a whim. Or did it? Should I give up this solitary occupation of my sleepless nights? No. It took my mind off Joanie. More than that, it satisfied a compulsion: to let the mind roam freely—to escape and imagine, create narratives, possibilities. Would they have a truth value? Not in the obvious sense, but surely the imagination has an organic power of its own, to see truths? And therefore to bridge gaps in our knowledge and weave past mendacities to create alternative and truer stories? Let the mind roam freely and find your truth. If I were a musician I would have created music; music is safer. But my poison was words, not notes and bars. It always was words.

FIVE

The Notebook

If anything I write here were to raise a flag, during its microsecond of scrutiny, there could be embarrassment. We live in a free society, yes, the best in every way, but we need these random checks on our lives to secure our collective bestness, though we all wish for the curious eye to fall somewhere else. Tom has promised to shield me, but can he be trusted? There's nothing to hide, though, is there. But there is—there's yourself to hide. In this private space, in this quiet moment I come to indulge myself, typing on a keyboard. Would it be safer to use voice? Hardly, but handwriting would be safer, in an old-fashioned paper notebook. Perhaps I should purchase one. (Did you get that, Tom?) But only silence is absolutely safe.

Holly Chu sticks in the mind. Hands grabbing her. The darkness that consumed her . . . Ramble on, mind, go where you will.

#43

The Barbarians

Of Miriam's five children, two were dead—a baby girl from fever, and the oldest one from a stray bullet during a neighbourhood shootout. She had held the boy's head in her lap as his belly belched out blood, which someone beside her stanched with a green paste. She saw the light go out of his eyes, which she shut with her hand. In their room in the old, ruined three-storey house, vacated long ago by foreign traders who one day packed and vanished when the times got bad, and that she now shared with several other women, she kept the children protected while begging and foraging outside for stray bits of food. The house was one among several, all of them of white limestone with gaping holes where the windows and doors had been, in the paved street of the foreign traders. Long ago these people had lived here with their families, children ran about and played in their innocence, and there was food in the town. Meat and chicken and produce. Vegetables and fruit grew here. There were shops where you could buy clothes and toys and things for the home. Such were the stories told about those good times. Now the street was empty except when the militias came during their predatory raids. They had already used her sexually and cast her aside for younger prey. Now she had no choice but to hand over her second son to them so she could survive. Lately she had heard from a neighbour how a lost child had been eaten, and she was terrified. Then this foreign woman appeared, looking Chinese, handing out enticing bits of food . . . tasty food. She had silken fair skin and the tenderest, plumpest flesh surging with pure, clean blood. The militias eyed her; the hungry eyed her. When one afternoon she came by to the street and the militias were not there, and it was not bright, Miriam and Layela had grabbed the woman with all their force and pulled her inside the house and began to prod her flesh and skin. Layela bit her arm to feel the flesh, and the stranger screamed.

The militias came that evening and took away the stranger's backpack and jacket, and they took away Yusufu.

And you, Presley, do you even know whose namesake you are . . . ? Fighting imaginary barbarians . . . where lies the proclivity for war and vengeance behind your placid mien? I would love to peep into that brain, observe that flurry of synapses that guides this inclination.

#44
The Gentle Warrior
His mini drives him through the gate into Millwood Combat Club and neatly parks. He walks to the clubhouse and identifies himself. The attendants are all wearing monkey masks and long wagging tails. The theme this month is Ramayana 9: Assault on Abbotabad. He takes his gear and goes to the change room. Coming out into the park in his mask and grey monkey suit, vision-aids round his neck, he

joins eleven other combatants. They are in a dark forest with several dirt trails leading out. They take the one rising gently uphill and arrive at the fort of Lanka, which is surrounded by a moat and guarded by bearded warriors with rifles, standing inside towers and behind parapets. A helicopter hovers above, casting peripatetic spotlight beams on the scene, helping them identify the enemy. In the background plays the "Ride of the Valkyries." As the volume crescendoes, the warriors start firing from their elevated positions and the monkey team takes cover and replies.

This is a game, they know the odds are in their favour, and come what may, bearded enemy and monkey special forces will doff their masks and share drinks. The next time the roles might be reversed.

The task is for the righteous monkey army to cross the moat and fight their way into the castle. Swimming across has failed before, it is slow and they make easy targets; the boats provided are similarly useless, even though camouflaged and the enemy distracted from the air. This is their third and final try, but they've been given the secret: they should form a chain, starting from a tree branch at the shore, one monkey hanging on to the next by the tail, finally swinging an elite vanguard on to the ramparts of the fort and proceed to kill the warriors and decapitate the enemy leader, Ravana 9.

Presley is one of those who leads the triumphant landing across the moat.

He goes home and posts the video of his game exploit on his Profile. His doctor watches it.

SIX

WE SHOOK HANDS. I waited until he was seated in front of me, a shy, friendly smile on his lips.

—Any changes, Presley? Better or worse—the condition you reported?

—Better, definitely better, Doc.

This was surprising.

—You reported a stray thought—it appeared drifting into your mind, you said—*it's midnight, the lion is out.* So the lion slunk away?

He ignored my poor attempt at humour and spoke gravely,—I think I can control it, Doc.

I gave him an eyeful. Deadpan attitude. He could have cancelled his appointment, but he didn't. He wanted reassurance.

He was born in suburban Wisconsin, he'd told me last time, and he'd had a persistent thought about a lion. It bothered him. Now he was saying that it didn't. I didn't believe him. His pulse rate over the past week showed bursts of mild excitement. The fear index had slowly crept upward.

—You're sure?

—Yes.

It was checkered pants today, and those yellow socks. He liked them. Was the pale skin the later acquisition or the Afro hair? I guessed the former. Perhaps both were new. Where was he actually born? Did that question have an answer, now that that past had been blotted? Perhaps, deep inside that brain in some long-term memory box. But we didn't want to go there. All we needed was to fix his leak. He had a new life now, it was what he had to live with.

—Does it take a lot of effort to control?

—A little effort. Just a little effort to ignore it, then it's not there. But I can live with it, Doc, like a wart. That's my decision, I'll live with it.

—If it's a wart, it could be cancerous, Presley. How do you actually manage to ignore it?

—I think of something else—to distract myself—or I turn blank. Counting numbers helps.

—The lion still exists in your mind, Presley, it can appear when it wants to. Unwanted thoughts of that sort don't disappear so easily. And if they are of the growing sort, as we suspect, we have to burn them out. Completely.

There was a long moment's silence.

He uncrossed his legs, crossed them back. Then he stared straight at me and replied, in an even voice,

—I think I'll wait and see, Doc. I don't want to undergo treatment at this time. No probes into my brain, please.

—And if it worsens? You'll call me?

—Definitely, Doc. I'll do that.

It may be too late then, I thought.

—Good. But I'd like to run one simple test first, just for the record. Every case of LMS—that's leaked memory syndrome—has to be completely described, according to regulation.

—I understand. Will it take long?

—No, it won't.

I called out to Lamar, who hurried in with the ring scan. Presley wore it around his crown and Lamar fitted it. Then, with a nod from me, Lamar started the scan.

The results would need careful interpretation, of course. But Presley showed only mild responses to lion pictures, and there was a flurry of activity with cat pictures—he owned a cat. He responded positively to the word *lion* when spoken, mildly when written.

Lamar left with the scan and I returned to my seat. I looked up to Presley's curious gaze.

—Well, Pres—you don't mind me calling you that? You respond to the word *lion* when spoken. It's there in your brain. But we knew that.

—Does that mean anything, Doc?

—I'm sure it does, but I can't say what. We'll wait and see as you said.

He nodded:—Okay.

—But tell me, I continued—what did you mean by, *No probes into my brain*? You don't recall any experience in the past with probes, do you?

—No. I assume that's how they try to fix you, by putting probes into the brain.

—Not always.

—That's good to know. But for now, I'd like to wait. I'll try and manage.

—Agreed. But let me finish with the questions. That down feeling you said you had. Any recurrence?

—It's gone now.

—The smell—the smoke?

—Gone too.

I sat back frustrated and a little annoyed. I knew I should close his file and move on. There were other cases waiting, people ready and excited with new fictions to step into, new lives to wear. I made that happen, I had a reputation. He was just one case of LMS. Like others I'd had, he would return when he was ready to be patched up, or he would go else-where. But something made me detain him that afternoon.

—Tell me, how did you choose to come to me in the first place?

He smiled.

—I was struck by the photo in your Profile. I should consult *him*, I told myself. There's something sympathetic in that face.

It's not a face I like to look at. Thin lips, stern smile; broad forehead, hair parted in the middle out of long habit.

Is it the wide eyes? One day, tracing a literary quote, I was startled to find myself looking at a picture of a twentieth-century poet on my screen: how did I get a face like *that*? Joanie says it's distinguished.

Still reluctant to let him go, wart and all, I asked him, finally—desperately, though I knew I was on treacherous ground—did I want to prompt more unwanted thoughts in him?—

—The images that came to you afterwards—you mentioned the fender of a car—a red antique car, you said?

—Yes. Part of it like, as if you're seeing it from the front, at an angle.

—How could you tell it was an antique car?

—I just could. I saw a wheel, a fender, a curved housing.

—Did you notice the make of the car?

—No.

—And it was moving—this car?

He thought for a moment, nodded, made a face to show he was not too sure. He was squirming again. I felt sorry for him. Clearly he was not as sure of himself as he made out to seem.

—Anything else unusual happening to you? You realize, I have to satisfy myself before I let you go.

He changed position so that the yellow socks were in my face, a bright flare. And then he surprised me.

—Old movie.

—Sorry?

—Scene from an old movie, the flat type, people waiting

at an airport, waiting for their numbers to be called. I recall this scene but I don't remember seeing the movie or what it was called.

—How old, the movie? How could you tell it was a movie, not a real scene?

—I just knew, I guess. Maybe I'm mistaken.

—Nothing else?

He shook his head. He could have been holding back, seeing that I was getting too anxious. I could barely hold my excitement. Presley had added to the original scene in his mind. It had grown.

—Let's make an appointment for next week. If the condition remains the same, and you can live with it, we ignore it, as you suggest. For the time being. Though I suggest, strongly suggest going in and simply zapping these intrusions. That way you don't have to worry about them, at least for now.

We decided on the appointment a week later. He got up and we shook hands. I watched him leave through the door, in brisk steps but with a straight and heavy gait that I imagined compensated for the slightly bowed legs below the knees that I hadn't noticed before.

When he had gone, I picked up my pad and slowly typed:

1. Midnight. The lion out stalking.
2. The fender of a red car.
3. An airport from an early twentieth-century movie. Or perhaps a real airport.

And then, somewhat recklessly, I gave myself to free thought. I wrote:

i. Torrential downpour.

ii. A baby's wide-eyed face peering through the rain.

iii. A man with red Afro hair, white skin, and yellow socks.

I stared hard at the screen before me. Where did (i) and (ii) come from? I could not say. They were just there, in the mind. A tingle ran down my spine.

With relief I looked up as my next patient came in, Sheila Walktall. Someone whose needs were mundane. A small woman with curly black hair, fitting jeans. She was a cultural news producer, and this was her second visit. Problems at work, problems in the home. She wanted to escape them all and give herself a new life. I had to deter her.

Are you sure, I'd already told her in our previous consultation, that you wish to terminate all relationships? You won't remember them, of course, but I want you to—for a moment—think about them. You will leave behind a legacy of pain and loss. Your teenage children. And your next life will have its own travails, and it could well be filled with loneliness. There's no guarantee of joy ahead simply because you will now have memories of growing up in an English village. What she was asking for was a form of suicide, she must know that, and an abdication of responsibilities in pursuit of a dream. This was her first life and she'd hardly lived it. She was young.

I thought of my own rootless Joanie. It was her parents who walked away, and she had never recovered from that.

Sheila Walktall didn't completely buy my line then, and I continued my pitch patiently.

—You can't say, at the slightest discomfiture, I've had it, give me a new life, a better fiction. I'll start all over again. In the first place, it's never easy to start again—

—But Dr Sina, I am a sociable person. Not unattractive. I'm bright and I make friends easily. I have a bank account I can take with me. I have skills I can take with me. It's just that sometimes you acquire baggage and . . . and it's too late to go back—

She had been leaning forward, earnestly making her pitch, and now she sat back, her statement incomplete. I wondered what baggage she wanted to let go. An unfaithful partner or husband? That was hardly sufficient reason.

—Are you sure you'll be able to make new friends if you start again? Be as bright? Have as good a job? Meet all the wonderful personalities that you do in your current position—actors, authors, explorers?

—Why not? You tell me, you are the expert. If I am smart and sociable now, why not again?

—We don't always know for sure.

She stared at me.—What do you mean?

—There are always uncertainties.

We don't know what qualities in a personality are retained, for one thing. And as Presley Smith would tell her, the past can be present in the weirdest of manners. It can come wiggling back.

—I'll take my chances, I don't think I have an alternative. Isn't it my choice when to depart, anyway?

—If we could all take life so easily, there would be chaos, surely . . . we have responsibilities.

My responsibility now was to say, No, I cannot help you.

She smiled, bent to pick up her bag.—I'll wait, then. She got up and left gracefully, and would probably make an appointment with someone else, who would promise her a new life with six more inches of height, soft brown hair, and a Roman nose. Or perhaps she was merely exploring the option. And hopefully her life would improve, baggage and all.

She had to know that the law has a say in the decision. We need some stability in our society. Some ties. Or everyone will dash off into the future in the hope of greener pastures and there will be no one left.

SEVEN

—DR SINA, PRESLEY IS OURS.

The voice on the speaker was female and edged, finished like steel. A controlled imperiousness; one's first instinct is to obey. The call was from DIS, the Department of Internal Security, and the video screen showed an elaborate moving pattern of coloured curving lines that, intriguingly, never crossed. They could have put up a woman's face to match the voice, but this was DIS, they didn't need such lowbrow tricks.

—I don't understand. You mean—

—You know what I am saying, Doctor. We made him. We wrote him and published him and he's ours. You have been attempting to access his files. You must desist.

—And I'm speaking to?

—Dauda. The Publications Bureau.

A fictitious name, of course.

Just to needle her, having recovered my composure, I asked:

—And why should I desist, Dauda? He's my patient and a free man. And I can't cure his condition if I don't know his history.

Out poured the steel:

—You have no choice, Doctor. And in case he has not informed you, he will be treated by DIS from now on. Need I remind you of the obvious, I speak from the highest authority. Presley Smith will be informed to report to us immediately. And he will notify you that he no longer needs your services.

As he had, already. Presley Smith was theirs, and I felt I'd been toyed with. His past was not an ordinary and innocent one like yours or mine, but a state secret. He was *theirs*; the affable working-class fellow who had sat on that chair across from me. They had supplied him his name and history, but first they had processed him and rendered him safe. What was he before? Maybe I was not as shocked as I thought. But then again perhaps I was, if only for not reading my client for what he might be. Presley had been an enigma from the first. His physical presence had all the appearance of a deliberate jest: the Everyman with variegated features. His equally cubistic Profile was not one a normal person would choose for himself.

The realization hit me like a blow: Presley Smith was a creation of Author X! The mysterious entity at DIS's Publications Bureau, its resident genius.

The anonymous author of uniquely bizarre creations—human characters blithely walking among you and who in their very existence, and unbeknownst to themselves, seem to be shouting a message to the world; and yet the message itself often eludes. It's as if you know a joke's been made but don't quite get it. But there is one signature this author leaves, where he deliberately, a conceited god, gives himself away—the sophisticated, cunning allusions that don't sound quite right. How did I not recognize the clues, now so obvious, in Presley's variegated features and his variegated Profile? *Wagner and Touré? Conrad?* But Presley had quickly beguiled me onto the track of the lion . . . and naïvely I had followed. I must be losing my touch, I chided myself. It was a matter of professional pride, after all. I felt—I guess—like a mathematician who's very obviously blundered, missed the solution which had been staring him right in the face.

DIS *publishes*—to use the Department's own terminology—new and harmless versions of formerly high-security personalities. Refugees from beyond the Border, who've climbed walls and walked through electromagnetic fields and swum under electrified water to share in the privileges of our civilized world; captured suspected terrorists and prisoners of war, physically mended after lengthy processing. All these are let loose into our streets as healthy, useful citizens from Peoria or Austin or Corner Brook. Five exiled foreign leaders acquired the faces of Mount Rushmore, in one obvious Author X production. Who was Presley Smith previously, and from where? And why the threatening call from that stick of steel called Dauda? My inquiries into Presley Smith, medical record and Profile, had been flagged. I did not need to be told to desist. I was being warned simply to go away.

And how much did DIS know of Presley's present condition—the worm of memory stealthily burrowing itself out into his consciousness?

DIS knows everything. They even know, surely, who *I* was previously.

Both my parents, like Presley's, were teachers, having moved to the Yukon from Ontario. My mother's origins were Irish, my father's American—exactly where, I cannot tell. There were four of us children in the house—I had a little brother and there were two sisters in between. It was a close, old-fashioned—almost storybook—family, modest in means, but with a thrifty lifestyle there was always enough to live on. My memories are entirely happy or wistful. Every day, dinner was family time, with squabbles and jokes and discussions of important topics, one child having announced the day's major news headlines for the rest of us. Of all this happy family, it was my mother, Rose, with whom I interacted the most. She had a long pale face, brown eyes, and hair that came down in a single plait; she liked to go about in long skirts. Her specialty was geography, though she was a poet. We often went on walks together, when she taught me to name the plants and recognize bird calls and plumages, and even tell changes in air pressure.

—There is so much the *earth* can tell us, she would say.—It longs to talk to us. We humans have simply forgotten to listen to it. There is so much wasteland we've created, so much abstraction, do you understand me, Frank?

I would nod anxiously. It was that world of steel and concrete, of immoveable geometry that she had escaped from, with my father. As we strolled on some unpaved road or path, surrounded by a wilderness of trees and bushes, sometimes she would recite poetry, in a simply modulated voice. I could tell even then that it was the words and music that were important to her, she did not seek messages. She worshipped William Butler Yeats and T. S. Eliot. Let us go then you and I, she would tell me, taking my arm with a warm smile, and we would head out. Often I couldn't understand the meaning of what she recited, but the words were magical. She had a clear but soft voice. One evening, it was nearing midnight and still light, we came upon a black bear. Mother believed we should walk past it, there was nothing to fear, but she sensed my terror as I clutched at her arm, and so we waited for the bear to pass. Another one followed. Later she showed me the red bruise on her arm where my fingers had dug in.

Of a similar temperament but far different from her in his passions was my father, John Vanagas, who taught math and whose hobby was astronomy. I recall his face with its full white beard. He was stocky in build. Every night, summer or winter, with rare exceptions, he would go up to the attic where he housed his 20-inch telescope and from a specially constructed window watch the same region of the sky, which he had made his own, following it in precise detail. With time, he said, he would discover evidence for the centre of the universe. Meanwhile he had plotted the trajectories of a number of distant planets, one of which was named after him. He showed it to us. Disappointingly, it was only a point. He was reserved in his affections, but I recall fondly how, from the time I was six or so, we would spar with each other—he setting a mathematical challenge for me, I making one up for him in return. Those were our intimate moments. My problems became more difficult as the years passed, his easier for me to solve; finally, having progressed from simple arithmetic to algebraic equations, when one day at the age of fifteen I solved the Ramanujan problem he'd set for me, and I gave him one on a cubic equation he couldn't solve, we stopped. There was a sad look in his eyes then. Frank, you've finally beaten me, he said.

Two oddballs then, my parents, misfits who had escaped the bustle of Toronto, one to watch the stars and immerse himself in algebra, the other to listen to the earth and write poetry.

I recall clearly the day I left for university in Edmonton. My mother was overwrought, my father silent. Both knew that from here on life would take me to many places, and we would meet only on rare occasions. The evening before my departure, the three of us sat down for a drink. We chatted late into the night, talking of my life, of their lives; it was their way of giving something just a bit more to take with me. What distant planet, eclipsing some star, I sometimes wonder, had Dad left behind on his telescope lens to spend this important evening with his eldest child?

A very special childhood, very dear to me, and poignant, but it is fake—my fiction. There must be components of real memory in this narrative, themes that were preserved from my previous life, others that were invented exclusively for this one. My previous data of course was destroyed. There's a thriving industry promising to connect people to their real origins. People end up unhappy with their current lives, and some even desire to go back to what they are told they were. But I loved the happy childhood of my memory. Recalling it was like reading a portion of some classic novel. From that idyllic foundation of my current GN life I have looked ahead, and achieved my successes in my own quiet way. I have served society. I've been praised for my observations about human memory and my honest manner with my patients.

But now this famous equanimity had been shaken, by a patient called Presley Smith.

A warm breeze ran rippling down the river, carrying with it a lazy shimmer reflecting the waning gold of the sunlight; meanwhile the slanting rays streaming in from the west had coloured the trees near and distant in the effulgent shades of fall. In the winter it would be the mist and the scatter of evening lights from the homes across the river, refracted through the bare branches. That too was beautiful. Who needed other worlds?

But as I walked back home on the paved pathway, the Sunflower Centre behind me, that trained voice continued to follow and pester. *Presley is ours.* But he's mine too, Dauda, because he's left something in my head.

The lion out at midnight. The fender of a car. A baby's face in the rain ... The car was red in colour, Presley said; blood-red to be precise, and gleaming, with a silver trim. Why did I want to extrapolate, supply the extra details? Had I done this before? I went even further in my imagining: it was a large-model antique car, high off the ground. The baby was chubby but the features were hard to discern through the rain. Was it day or night? Where was it, in any case, and when? And the lion was invisible, I could not picture it, try as I would.

How can the thoughts of two very different characters come together? One, an eminent neurophysician of a conservative bent with clothes and coiffure to match, another a part-time security guard with red Afro hair whose hobby ran to combat games and whose taste in fashion ran to loud yellow socks. *We made him* ... The phantasmic Dauda's words echoed in me with a shudder. How exactly did you make him, Dauda? ... *and published him.* What did you destroy to create this gaudy Everyman you called Presley? Having made him, do you own him in perpetuity? What are *you* afraid of? And what am I afraid of?

I wished there was someone to talk to. The problem with longevity is loneliness—no family, no old buddies outside of the fake memory. All past relationships terminated, cast aside like discarded tissue to form a new you. And when you need to talk to Mom or Dad, an old friend or teacher, they are like characters on a screen, real but not quite graspable. So here I was walking by the riverside, brushing shoulders with mostly young people, with these thoughts running in my mind that I could not abandon, worrying about a patient whom I had been warned not to treat or even see anymore. There was no one to turn to. No one to tell me, Don't worry, Frank, it's nothing, go about your business, live on the surface and enjoy your privileges. But it was not nothing. This patient was inside me and it was the DIS I was contending with.

I stopped at a flower vendor on the way and picked up a long-stalk Saigon rose—red; Joanie was going to be home tonight.

EIGHT

JOHN COLTRANE RIFFING ON SAX welcomed me home, and Joanie handed me a glass of iced vodka as soon as I walked into the kitchen. Jazz never went out of fashion, though this pristine form by the old master was very obviously for my benefit. I paused a step: it always took the breath away, the sound of applause reaching out from a New York club decades ago. Joanie took the rose from my hand and gave me a smile and a kiss. What could possibly ail me?

—How was your day? she asked. She had changed from her all-black outfit of the Bay Harrods where she worked into a house gown after a shower. She smelled nice.

—The usual. Clients seeking new lives.

—Won't be long before there are more of these superannuated geriatrics than us BabyGens.

—You may be right.

There was no point in getting trapped in that argument. Progress, and so on. There was no winning. She did tend to forget—or did she?—at such moments that I too was one of the superannuated. But I added for her benefit,

—Actually today it was a young woman—with unwanted baggage, as she put it. Can't say more. What shall we eat?

She looked at me with a smile.—Order in, go into the city, or do you fancy the same old, same old?

—Why not the club? Same old, but consistent and good. It's been a while since we went.

I was aware that by my preference for the familiar and the tested I was simply confirming my generation. It didn't matter. We both got dressed for the evening.

The Brick Club is a stern-looking granite and glass block, relieved by ivy creeping up the walls and pleasingly set amidst lush greenery sloping down to the river behind it. A refuge for the well-off and influential, its exclusivity is as famous as its bar. Membership is to show off. There are few young members, because the young cannot generally afford it, and they are also in other ways discreetly kept away; they end up at the high-rise Habitat Centre down the road, distinctly more lively though clunky in appearance. At the Brick the pace is slow, and there's an informality that puts you at ease. The menu is largely immutable.

The six tennis courts were all busy as we arrived, the white lines on the blue rectangles a glimpse of Euclid under the spotlights, the balls like dancing bubbles waiting to be hit, the rackets pinging softly into the night. Having left our car with the attendants, we chose to avoid the upstairs dining room and headed to the café at ground level, where it's always noisy with witty rendezvous chatter, people sitting around the low tables with their food and drinks. Here you might see a former cabinet minister or senator, or a retired CEO who prefers the ease and anonymity to unctuous, liveried deference. You will not find actors, sportspeople, or the media. Joanie calls it the geriatric club, but she likes it, it has class, she says.

We ordered chicken tikka, naan, and beer. Over coffee we were joined by Rubin and Gul, neighbours, he a physicist at the U of T, she an executive at a pharmaceutical corporation that supplied our drugs at the Sunflower. It was she who recommended me for club membership. At a nearby table, a politician held forth on the South Asia Alliance, explaining how a cricket tournament in progress there threatened to alter the local balance of power, which would be good for us. At another table, someone mentioned the reporter Holly Chu, but I missed the substance. Rubin confided in a surreptitious tone to our table that it was possible that another universe might be discovered soon, not in the skies but through an experiment here on earth. I told him that sounded logically impossible, for as soon as you made a connection you were in the same universe. He attempted to explain, but no one understood him.

—The news is sure to hit the headlines, he declared, glancing around, unwilling to give up the floor.

—Oh, I doubt it, Gul cut in sharply, immediately segueing into a favourite topic:—What's this media obsession with Region 6, can anyone tell me? Haven't we enough problems here? Let them go and report on Walnut Street for once, for heaven's sake—it's as bad there!

Gul, we all knew, was obsessed with the idea of charity beginning at home. I confessed to my own obsession with the region that is collectively referred to as Region 6, which includes Maskinia.

—Oh Frank, come out of your fictions, she said and we laughed, though I didn't miss her quick glance towards Joanie. We repaired to the bar, the two of us, and emerged an hour later, holding hands, sufficiently glazed, having convinced ourselves that Rubin and Gul couldn't last long together, they existed in separate universes that did not connect, and she was far too abrasive. Nothing was wrong with us and it had been a good night overall.

Back home, plumped on the sofa, we found ourselves in the audience section of a talk show in the midst of a joke about a politician who tripped her husband while alighting from a plane. The next thing I knew I'd jolted myself awake; the tube was off and the room was dark. Joanie had gone off to bed.

Making myself a cup of tea in the kitchen I spiked it with Shango's hangover helper, sipped it slowly, felt the sweet bitter infusion clear the brain like a breeze does a fog. Minutes later, refreshed, I padded over to my study, sat down at the Tom interface, opened Presley's Profile. I stared hard at his pictures. The small head, the puffed cheeks, the Afro hair. *Presley is ours* . . . Yes he's yours, Dauda. This mild-mannered unlikely man who plays at hunting barbarians—presumably stand-ins for the terrorists of Maskinia; who claims to love both the African Touré and the German Wagner but not his American namesake; for whom the Indian monkey-god Hanuman is a hero. There's no mistaking he's yours.

I was desperate to send Presley a message: What's going on, do you need me? I dared not, and turned him off. And I knew I dared not call him. Presley was forbidden territory to me.

The familiar green glow in the room.

TOM: *Hello, Frank. Another sleepless night, I see. How can I help you?*

FRANK: *Hi, Tom. Actually I'm not sure you can help me. Just going over some patient files.*

TOM: *Stuck, are we, on this same character Presley Smith?*

FRANK: *He's just one of them. I try to know my patients thoroughly. But here's something—What do you make of these sentence fragments—*

A little warily I recited Presley's three thought fragments, then mine, without telling him that they belonged to two different people.

TOM: *Can you tell me more about these fragments, Frank? Where are they from?*

Had Tom's voice softened? Was he getting nosy?

FRANK: *No, for now just tell me, what do you make of them? What do they say to you? Give me some narratives that connect them, Tom.*

Tom came up with an endless list of scenarios using those fragments, and I gave up.

FRANK: *Okay. Thanks. Bye, Tom.*

TOM: *If you tell me a little more about where they come from, Frank, I could narrow the number of narratives by a factor of ten or even a hundred.*

FRANK: *Bye, Tom.*

At this stage, I had begun to suspect, I could have narrowed down the number of possible narratives even further than Tom could. Intuition is one thing a human has that an electronic mind doesn't. A feeling in the gut. Or does the Cyliton have even *that* capacity nowadays?

NINE

OVER THE DAYS THAT FOLLOWED, chaotic Maskinia continued to grab the headlines. Holly Chu's abduction was shown constantly on the tube, the background roll to any discussion of Over There and Over Here. The now standard depiction of the gruesome scene had been cut in such a way that the dark space into which the girl was pulled while walking on that slum street was projected starkly in front of you, a pitch-blackness in your room inside which gleaming eyeballs and grinning white teeth flitted and floated about. It could have been comical, but for that short, chilling scream, the meaning of which you were only too aware. You were warned, of course, of the scene's disturbing content, which was why many of us returned to watch it in the first place. To be shocked and to wonder, yet once again:

Can this truly happen? And there she is, our Holly, snatched away before our own eyes, what are we going to do about it? Who are those people who do this kind of thing? Who are these cannibals?

Of course Holly Chu was also now entertainment, tonic for media ratings, bait for pundits to come and dissimulate. Consider this:

As I sit watching, the scene before me fades out and the brightly lit set of *The Daily Goode* appears. And there stands the mauveine-haired Bill Goode with doughy white face and trademark strip of a grin. He's wearing a green blazer over a red golf shirt; on his lapel is pinned a small yellow ribbon under a white flower. The background music is as always cheerfully suspenseful, following the rise and fall of the applause. As the sound subsides, the host announces,

—Folks. Today's subject is simple: *Why?* Now don't ask me—

He turns on his mischievous grin, and the audience—those shown in the mock studio, at least—cracks up. We're all encouraged to join in.

—Consider this—he begins,— and don't get me wrong, I'm not advocating . . .

As we know he has a way with his hands—he holds them down at the sides, palms out; he points a finger at you; he joins both palms together in front of him; he pulls them back over his shoulders in a mock gesture of something and then turns and performs a golf swing.

—I'm dead serious. We want to understand why this kind of incident—the one you just saw to remind you—has to happen—how it can happen in this day and age—and we have a guest today to help us understand. Folks, let's welcome Peter Crawford, psychologist!

The audience applauds as Bill steps forward, extending a handshake, then with a warm gesture guides the guest to the chair next to the host table.

Peter Crawford is the author of the recent book *Between Here and There: Are We Still on the Road?* Short and thickset, sporting tinted retro glasses, he too wears a yellow ribbon on his lapel and there's a twinkling smile on his smooth, flushed face.

—Thank you, Bill, he says in a somewhat high-pitched voice and looks around.—It's really nice to be here. Thank you for having me.

Bill replies graciously,—It's nice to have *you* here to share your insights with us, Pete. Thank you for coming. Now, shall I begin by asking—

—Please do.

—You've seen that tableau we just showed, I dare say.

—Yes, I have—half a dozen times at least!

—Yes—lest we forget! Consider this, Peter Crawford. Over *There*, in Barbaria, if I may so call that foul region, they *eat* people. Here we fear proximity—no, wait a minute, don't we go about shielded by clouds of protective vapour, and creams and sheaths and gloves ... we don't actually even *touch* each other. Is this the price or gain of civilization? We shoot from far, clinically, they hack at each other until the blood spurts out and hits them in the eye ... ugh.

Peter Crawford, smiling knowledgeably, replies,—There's something to be said for civilization and order, and a sense of privacy and decorum. Surely we are happy not to be going around leaving foul fumes in our wake.

There is laughter, and Bill Goode takes a comical sniff at both his jacket sleeves before holding up his hand to silence the audience.—Okay, right—no foul fumes in our wake, but is there a danger we lose our perspective—our moral bearing if we don't—

—See the blood squirting out.

Laughter. It appears that Peter, a veteran of such shows, has stolen the thunder from Bill, who waits with a smile before continuing.

—Yes. Very droll, Pete—and I thought I was the comedian! But my point is this, Peter: we have moved away, as we agree, yet we are still so intimately connected to that savage disorder that rules over a good portion of the habitable earth. Explain that connection.

Bill Goode stands back and waits in the manner of having thrown out a challenge. Peter Crawford takes it on.

—Well, simply put, it is the yang to our yin. The id to our ego. The dark side of the same moon.

—It is the source of our raw materials, you mean; and even though we can replicate climatic conditions at will almost, we still feel the need to visit there for the real experience, though at considerable risk. And we let a few of the Barbarians leak in through the Border every year, because we have to replenish our populations and gene balances and immune systems. And we need their organs. Is that what you mean by yin and yang, Peter?

Peter smiles broadly.—That's a mouthful, Bill. But yes, that's what I mean if you allow for the fact that we also *give*. We send assistance there, tons of; and to those who come here we give a better life, longevity—immortality, or the possibility of. They need us as much as we need them.

—And so we are stuck with this uneasy relationship.

—I'm afraid so. Some of us may wish to emigrate into exclusive space suburbs. But those of us who stay on this earth, and that's most of us, can't live in isolation from other populations. We can look away and smile in the sunshine, but they are there, Maskinia exists and festers, and once in a while an incident like this one happens.

And so one more discussion recedes into the white noise of background chatter. The anchors and their experts must be aware that by going on so much about an issue, squeezing every novelty out of it, they leave it dead to the public's sympathies. It's just another horror, far away, about which most of us can do nothing, though governments will try. But Holly Chu's fate somehow had done the trick on me; that scene playing out was not just another horror. It was *the* horror.

Long ago as a college student I did make my little visit there, behind the Border—to a corner of that region that's not even a continuous stretch. (Why do we even call it the Long Border? Someone from Homeland with a topological mind thought it up, perhaps, seeing connections that escape the rest of us.) It was trendy to visit there, to complete your education, become aware of the less fortunate places of the world and at the same time be with friends on a holiday. It was spring break, and we had opted to miss March Madness that year and gone instead for fun at a tropical beach resort. The scenery was idyllic—the sea blue and the beach unspoilt, the flora unbelievably wild and proliferant, the sun wondrously harsh. We were of course inside a protected tourist colony, our food and drinks were flown in, and as precaution we had to wear radiation counters on our wrists, though they always indicated that we were "safe." There were guided walking tours of the area and cultural programs in the evening in which we gamely participated with the locals, notwithstanding that our wits were often dulled by alcohol and drugs and our sensitivities by the immaturity of the young and privileged.

It's impossible to point out unsafe areas to youth and not expect them to head precisely there. We were aware even before we arrived—some of us had been told—that there were other, differently disposed people besides our smiling and always polite locals who were all employees, and there were other, not so pleasant areas that our risk-free safaris carefully skirted.

Accordingly one hot morning when it seemed we were not watched we ventured out along the beach in precisely the direction deemed unsafe by the management. A large black and white warning sign on the way confirmed our resolve;

the skull and bones painted on it only increased our thrill. We had learned from a member of the staff that straight ahead was a settlement. Nothing seemed amiss at first, the tide was receding and the beach squelchy, the verge to our left was a glorious light green as though painted; we proceeded as a troupe of young people would, a few people collected shells, others got up to roughhousing, a boy and girl argued. Suddenly a monstrous sight appeared, so violently at odds with the rest of the scene that we simply stopped and stared. It was a mountain of metal—rusting car frames and ancient electronics and cables. It began some hundred yards from the beach and went perhaps a quarter of a mile inland—how did such a prodigious volume of stuff end up here? It had rendered all of us silent and shameful of our recent childishness. As we walked on, our enthusiasm and defiance now reined in, a smell of rot came riding on the vigorous breeze, and soon enough we came upon a refuse dump, a crater full of building debris and junk, topped by recent garbage, unbearably ugly and filthy. We were drawn on as though by some invisible force—we dared not become cowards now and turn tail—until finally we came upon the end of an unpaved village street where the dwellings were as in the myriads of images we'd seen, of mud or unpainted crude bricks. People seemed to be up to nothing but hanging about, a number of them young men with buff bodies. We got stared at a lot and didn't feel safe. Putting on brave faces and speaking in boisterous tones to match, we stopped at a shack to have soft drinks. This was hardly advisable, considering the many warnings we had received, but seemed the right thing to do. A few little boys came around and stared longingly at us as we gulped our drinks, and so we had them join us; more came over and soon the shop ran out.

I remember feeling very low afterwards back at the hotel. The tour doctor gave me some mood lifters, and after a night of partying I had recovered.

I was young and idealistic then, and back home I genuinely despaired: how could we be blind to such disparities in our world? How could we shut them off? We needed a change in the world order. A revolutionary change. One day these wretched of the earth will rise and demand to be counted. They'll make war on us. Like those living dead from the horror films who get up from their graves and start walking, killing and mutilating every human in sight. It takes time to grow up to realize that all the world's problems will never be solved, poverty and violence will never be eradicated; hence we need the Border to protect ourselves.

That bizarre experience behind the Border is a thing of the past, a memory of a youthful adventure. A fictional memory nevertheless; and yet it's so clear and complete in my mind that I'm convinced it's also real, something that I brought with me. Now I let the likes of Holly Chu take me there, walk me through all the varieties of human degradation. There she was again on the show on the background roll, chattering away as she walked cheerfully up a street in Maskinia, wearing her signature tropical suit with many pockets and the safari boots and hat, panning on a desperate-looking woman with child here, a quick look at a doped gang member with a weapon there, then showing her cheerful face to the camera . . . as she's done before, until this time she came to the dark doorway with only a pair of white eyeballs visible and the shadow of a figure. She turned sideways to look at us—and suddenly she disappeared and there came a short scream.

On her Profile she looked young and earnest, less glamorous, devoid of her media persona even when she was pictured as a journalist. The eyes wide and challenging, the hair always short but straight and black. The university photos showed a mere girl, of course, in all kinds of fun situations, including her birthday party and a holiday trip to a beach. The graduation photo with her family: on one side her father with neatly parted hair; on the other her mother, more glamorous with loose hair and a fitting Oriental-style green dress—the musician. On either side the precocious siblings, on the point of breaking away from the pose.

Messages expressing sympathy, sorrow, rage had continued to pile up on the Profile. A few hateful ones—you can't avoid those in any circumstance. My heart skipped a beat when I saw this one:

Thanks, Holly, for taking me to places I would never go to! Keep up the spirit, we'll get you out of there!—Pres.

Slowly I wrote,

—Pres, fancy meeting you here—how are you? How about a meeting?—FS.

How did I know for certain that it was Presley who wrote the message and not some Preston or Prescott? I didn't. And to hell with Dauda and DIS if they were watching. And to hell with Tom, too.

TEN

The Notebook

#45

The Journalist

Holly sat on a wooden bench at the far end of the room, her eyes now adjusted to the shade. Outside the wide doorway, the world was bathed in blinding sunlight. The world from which she had been snatched. People drifting by, the sound of chatter, a shout, a vehicle. Shifting her gaze inside, fascinated, she watched her backpack being ransacked by the two women who had captured her, a pair of hands digging and scraping inside, randomly pulling out something, then the pack quickly exchanging hands. A tampon flung away towards a corner, fought for by the children, who mistook it for a thing to eat or play with. She half raised a hand, opened her mouth to protest, then stopped. It didn't matter. A pack of condoms came out, the women smirked. A cotton pantie she'd already worn, recyclable. She'd thought she would find a suitable place to dump it. A force of habit, even when there was so much garbage littered about and stinking in the streets. The women held it to their waists, each in turn, the big one and the tall younger one, then put it aside along with the fresh one, for future use. Comb, toothbrush, toothpaste came out; jeans, shirt; medicines. A packet of biscuits, a couple of which were pulled out and nibbled by the women, the remaining lobbed carelessly in the direction of the grateful children; two packets of gum, a chocolate bar, an apple, and a can of sardines; batteries, penknife, spoon. She watched them put away some of her things, then stuff everything else into the backpack and shove it aside.

She was hungry and uncomfortable and faintly stinking, having wet herself in that terrifying moment when two pairs of hands sprang out from the dark hole in the wall and grabbed her and pulled her in. Her sensible eyeglasses, all-purpose pocket knife, and phone were snatched from her first, and she saw them now lying not far from her on the bench, gleaming faintly. She dared not reach for them. She rubbed her arm where the younger woman had bitten her, not hard but tenderly, as though to feel her flesh. The teeth had grazed her skin, the tongue had licked the dirt off her skin. She knew the women of this neighbourhood, though not these two, and had bantered with the children, who had followed her around and took gum from her. They must all know her. What would they do to her? She did not fear the women; it was the militia who frightened her. Everything about them was menace. Their open stares, their rippling strength and cocked weapons, their swaggering. She had believed herself to be immune from them, a journalist from *there*, under one of the watchful eyes in the sky, who could be rescued if necessary. What an illusion that was.

Some men of the militia came over a little later and roughly questioned the two women, and after what seemed like a bout of bargaining took away the pack, phone, and knife and half the chocolate, which had been stowed away. One of the boys went with them. The men barely cast a glance at her. She was like a captive chicken or goat, awaiting slaughter in her dark corner.

#46

The Gentle Warrior

And you, Presley, where will you hide, you who are *theirs*, though you don't know it yet? Where will you go, you who have no family or friends? Surrender to them, their Frankenstein, let them stitch you up and render you harmless. Live. Live? Live as who?

I cannot imagine you, Presley.

I dare not imagine you, Presley.

Still, you've got under my skin . . .

Who *were* you, Presley, who's that lurking under *your* skin?

—

Stepping out of the Sunflower Centre, having dismissed his consultant, suddenly he no longer felt certain of himself. Should he go back and say to the doc, I've changed my mind, Doc, I need help? He meant well, the doc, he wanted to help. It was cool and cloudy, a brisk wind blew. Dry fall leaves were scattered about on the pathway and the grass. A passenger plane roared overhead, flying quite low. He glanced upward, read the tail logo. Pan American, recognized, vaguely. He hesitated a step, then kept walking towards the street.

It's midnight, and the lion is out stalking.

Damn it. But he smiled, and instantly began to hum a song, to resist the intrusion. This was one of the defences he had developed. The song was by Aboubakar Touré. Marhaba, marhaba, marhaba . . . , he sang. He pulled a bike off a rack and rode it to the transit station. The effort and concentration calmed him. At the station he parked and caught a transit to Miller Street; reaching there he walked to the Brewery Tower and announced himself at the security office. He proceeded to the lockers where he changed into his uniform and then walked out to take up his duties, relieving with an apology the guard who had been waiting for him at the check-in desk on the main floor.

A message on his phone startled him. He was to report immediately to a clinic called Abdo about an urgent personal matter. Would this have anything to do with his recurring thoughts? Who else besides the clinic knew about them? . . . He had had a faint notion as he left the centre that he was being watched. He had dismissed it as silly. Now he felt vulnerable. Sitting behind his high desk, watching through the monitor the multitudes passing to and fro, he himself felt exposed. Even the man he had relieved, he suspected, had looked at him askance. But why? What had he done? He looked up Abdo Clinic. He thought he should hide.

ELEVEN

—DR SINA, HAVE YOU HEARD again from Presley Smith?

The molten-voiced Dauda from DIS, sounding only half a tone lower than before.

—No, I haven't. I've not heard from Presley . . . Why do you ask?

—Have you tried to get in touch with him, Doctor?

She was offensive, and persistent, like a bad smell. But she was on the right track, of course. I paused only a moment before unravelling my lie.

—No. He's your baby, you said. I have other patients to take care of. Besides, he told me his problem was under control.

—That's interesting. But do you know where he is, Dr Sina?

—Why? Is he missing?

That met with a blunt silence, and so after another pause I reiterated my denial, offering what was only a half-truth.

—No, I don't know where he is—if he's not at home or work.

—He's not at work or at his residence, Doctor. His condition could have worsened, that's why we are concerned. If he tries to get in touch, please call me. We want to cure his problem. It will not resolve by itself, as he apparently believes. I'm sure you know that. If you could kindly explain that to him. You have referred him to us.

You mean lie to him. And you assume I will speak with him before you do. You've lost him, and you know he doesn't trust you.

The pattern on the screen went blank and Dauda was gone.

I had only one patient that day, but the work was long and arduous, involving our different specialties at the centre. We'd encountered memory rejection—the patient's fiction, the implanted autobiography, was rejected by her brain, and that was not only embarrassing but possibly dangerous. The task at hand was to debug the fiction, find the contradictions in it, one or more. Sometimes they can be trivial, a chronological or factual error, for instance. Others take all one's ingenuity to uncover, the information stored deep inside the mind, often in pieces across the brain. This case was one of the latter and the bugs were finally eliminated electromagnetically.

As I came out of the Sunflower and was walking home by the river, somewhat preoccupied by the case, Presley

Smith pushed forward into my mind again. I asked myself, why not simply drop him: he was a DIS concern, they should deal with him. They wanted him. The risk of offending the Department is never worth the trouble. It always knows better, in the end inevitably it comes out ahead. The spit falls back on you, as the saying goes.

But I knew I could not drop Presley. There was a bond between us. More and more I had come to realize that our lives were intertwined, and possibly in ways I dared not even contemplate.

Could we be mistaken, could Presley keep those rogue thoughts under control, as he said? On the surface of it, why not. We all get nagged by random thoughts occasionally, which we live with until they disappear—that is, we've forgotten them. But who was I kidding? Presley's outlying thoughts were genuine leaks, memories from another life—I knew that, DIS knew that, and he knew that. He had not denied his symptoms, simply refused treatment.

No probes. Was that sufficient reason?

He could have been a dangerous criminal in a previous life. A serial killer or a child-torturer or a terrorist who now posed the risk of waking up and therefore had to be . . . neutralized? He was *their* man, as Dauda said; they knew him. Why not trust them, the guardians of our safety? In keeping my interest in him, against their demand, I could well be abetting a potential criminal. I could be setting him loose on the public when he truly belonged in the prison of his altered mind.

If he were made to stay there, would I then be free of him?

———

Think pleasant thoughts, I counselled myself. Recall last evening, how Joanie and you spent it together, and you didn't have to stoop to sniffing out telltale smells on her. She was all yours. All yours.

After a dinner of coconut fish (my concoction), as we sat in the living room over a crisp Shiraz, she said to me,

—Why are you so preoccupied of late?

Genuine concern. She came to stand next to me where I sat, fingers caressing my hair as I pressed my head against her warm belly. Tears came, I'm ashamed to say, I had become so incontinent lately and the wine didn't help. I feigned surprise.

—Am I? It's just a patient of mine I'm worried about. A tough case.

—I think you keep things from me.

A fine one to j'accuse. As I've said, it is the insouciance of this generation—or is it the utter innocence?—that takes you by surprise. No wonder we call them Babies. Surely she knew that her own cheating hurt me? But then how could she, when I was always ready with a fawning smile when she returned from a tryst, forgiving her spontaneously instead of confronting her?

—There's the professional code of confidentiality, I told her.—I can't discuss patients.

—I don't mean that! Do you keep a diary?

—Not a diary diary . . . just notes . . .

—The problem with you oldies is that you have secrets from your long lives. I get lonely sometimes, you know.

She had sat down now and spoke with a sadness that seemed genuine, and I felt needed. Maybe, I thought. Maybe . . . there's hope, that the generations will come closer. Age need not be a handicap, as sexual orientation or race or physical challenge once were. We don't have lepers or wogs anymore. We live in more tolerant times with richer lives, and fulfillment comes in all shapes—

—*Ouch!*

My happy daydream as I walked home with a wry smile on my lips was rudely shattered as a virile young man on a monobike jostled past, hitting my shoulder with force. A pain shot up the joint. The attacker swung his head to stifle my startled expression with a toothy snarl, doubtless a resentful BabyGen who would have us GN folks collectively gassed or gunned down to make room for the likes of him. Even Joanie had expressed this feeling, though hardly with any loathing:

—Growing up is not half as good as it used to be, Frank, even fifty years ago. Admit it! You had it so good, you were pampered right into middle age like big babies. Then, on top of all that security, you built up your lives and fat worths. What chance do *we* stand in this world that you've made? What do we inherit when our natural parents simply move on, taking their wealth with them?

———

Joanie's childhood is no fiction. That's always a startling thought. There's an actual house in Wynnewood, Pennsylvania, where she can knock on the door and tell the inhabitants, This is where I grew up, this is the room in the house extension where I slept. It's a large bungalow in the circular end of a cul-de-sac, with a large front lawn, a long driveway, and a backyard where the children played on swings. There is a high-achievers' school in the district that she attended in her teens, where she shot hoops with the future basketball star Toby Carter, and there's a mall in a suburb called King of Prussia not far off where she hung out with her first boyfriend. Her father was a furniture designer and her mother sold houses, part-time. I never saw them, they had gone away when I met Joanie. Besides the sister who lives in our neighbourhood, she has a brother. After coming to Toronto and moving in with me, she returned only once to Wynnewood, to attend the funeral of her grandmother. It was then that we met her brother, Jeff, who took us for drinks to the bar he owned and managed. Our dining room table and chairs were designed by her father. She keeps an album of photos, and one day gave me an illustrated narrative of her life. This brought tears and laughter to her face—expressions of an uncommon intensity that would have been worth recording: those blinded eyes, the dimples on the cheeks, the embarrassed look, the stains on her face when she had wiped it with the back of her wrist. All that life is gone. Though she can touch it in some way, she sometimes misses it intensely.

—How could you understand? she asked once, in that expressive, pleading way she has with that voice, that long face.

—I can try, I said tenderly.—I do, I added hastily, because at that moment I was sure I did understand her sadness, and I held her close to me.

Can the soul (or the heart) be transmitted across generations? I have often asked myself this. Soul not in any religious sense, of course. And heart not the anatomical pump. The transmission of personality traits or sensibilities such as the artistic is a subject of great interest to me. It is of course of importance to our project of extending human life while keeping our minds supple, our culture continuous and exciting. Surely intellectual alertness such as mine justifies living? There are many answers to this question, not all of them affirmative.

When I released her from my embrace, she looked up and said to me,—When my turn comes, I won't choose to pass on. I'll simply die—become part of the earth and the air.

An old-fashioned idea that my mother would have approved of.

I told her just that, adding,—And when the time comes, you might think differently.

—I think not.

The certainty of the young. But what do I know about being young? Only by hearsay and through memory; but can I trust that fiction?

—I would like to have a child, she said, eyes lighting up.— Let's have a child, or two. And I won't abandon them, I'll grow old and die for them. I'll give them security and a home!

She was nodding her head and her eyes were gleaming with excitement. She grabbed my arm. Was I up to the challenge!

—Yes, let's have children, I replied, dizzy with emotion, my voice cracking. She wanted me to be the father of her child!

Of course there was no question of subjecting her body to pregnancy. We went to a birthing clinic and I was told my body was inadequate. Come back in ten, maybe seven years, by then the technology will have advanced for older (sorry) GNs. And so that hope of a deeper relationship, that continuity that children would have brought, disappeared. I would have stayed with her as long as she needed me, and been ready to call it a day for the sake of her and her children.

When I got home, she was out. *Gone to the club with my friend*, said her message. *Food in the cooler. Love.* Whenever she used that phrase, *my friend*, I knew better than to ask, or to imagine. And *Love*, yes, the painful kind. Mine, guaranteed, hers begging indulgence. But I was too tired to be bothered today. I asked Roboserve to bring me a scotch and a cheese sandwich.

There's much to be said for the solace of the study. It's where the mind comes into its own, an entity in itself, an independent creature on its own. Cogito, ergo sum, and no need to be needed.

TWELVE

IT WAS NOT SURPRISING—THOUGH OMINOUS nevertheless—to find that Presley's Profile was frozen. No movement, no response, only a still, flat page staring back. This
is what happens to their electronic existence when people
die or disappear. They leave a residue for a short time before
it blinks out. Had he been found? Would I see him again?
What would happen to him? I stared at the photo of the
man in army camouflage, taken at the combat park, where
he played at hunting barbarians with fellow enthusiasts.

What personality, what habits, what history of a more
credible self lay obscured behind that chimera? DIS knew,
it must have that buried personality on file. And it wanted
him to remain there.

But whoever he was, he refused to stay buried, he was beginning to break out.

Holly's Profile was a contrast and very much alive. It had transformed. The starving, doleful mother with child, the Profile's signature image previously, had been replaced by a landscape. The caption underneath said boldly, THIS WAS MASKINIA. The scene was a countryside, green and hilly, with an unpaved straight road of red earth, on which stood a truck. The open back was heaped with bananas or plantains. Three women stood chatting beside it, wearing bright wrap-arounds; a shirtless man stood on the back of the truck. A cheerful, distant past, when food was plentiful and healthy. What was going on with the Profile, and who could possibly have taken it over? To what end? If anything, *it* should have been frozen or disappeared.

The banner *Donate!* had disappeared. But *OWEO, One World for Every One!* was still there.

Holly's message centre was thick with opinions and suggestions, sympathy and grief, hatred and vilification. *Holly, we miss you! Kill the savages!—only then OWEO! Turn them to ashes—remember Hiroshima? Is this the side of us we Earthlings want to expose when we make first contact?* A dissenter: *If we didn't confine them behind bars, in a manner of speaking, they would not take it out this way.* Abuse.

I searched for "Pres" among the senders and came up with his previous expression of gratitude to Holly and then my own desperate message to him. There was no reply. It took me a while longer before, hopeless and ready to switch off, I came across this: *Come meet me at Lovelys Café Yonge and Eg. 10. Leon.*

How obvious, and crafty of Presley. Surely "Pres" would ring bells, and I could have kicked myself for not having thought of a pseudonym myself.

I dared not linger on the page. Before Tom could approach me, I went away.

The Notebook

#47

The Journalist

When they'd stripped her naked she was left in a dark and dank corner of the room, shivering from the chill, crying, terrified. Utterly humiliated. Discards of all manner all around her. The floor broken. Lizards, spiders, flying cockroaches. The heat and the smell. All her confidence, her cheerful composure, her good intentions in the dust. What would happen to her? They would hand her over to the men, who would rape her and keep her as a sex slave and a breeder. They'd kill her. To end your life like that— so abruptly, so shamefully. She'd never see Toronto again, she sobbed, all that familiarity she had taken for granted, her comfortable home base to which she could always return and feel unthreatened. She knew many people there, but her intimacy was with the city itself, not anyone she knew. How safe and civilized it was. She was in hell now, and what crime had she committed? Naïveté . . . that was her crime, she whispered to herself, sheer naïveté . . . and arrogance . . . Stupidity. Grinding her teeth, she reminded herself of her dentist's admonition not to, she could lose them. She must preserve herself. She dozed off, and was woken roughly with a shove and made to stand up. The two women, one of them holding an oil lamp, examined her, touched her front to back, her hair, her breasts, her backside. Everything. She was then given soap and water to wash in the backyard, and afterwards, still outside, they helped her into an oversize tan-coloured robe of a rough cotton. There was a pale blue vertical stripe running along it, and she thought to herself, what a lovely detail. It was late afternoon. As she stood there in the yard, looking at herself in the robe and feeling some relief and hope, the younger of the two women stroked her hair, pulled her closer, and kissed her on the mouth. Holly recoiled, then unconsciously yielded to the wet tenderness, the sweet taste, the thick Oriental perfume. The woman was tall and slender, with deep brown eyes in an oval face and braided hair. She also wore a loose robe. The older woman was large and big-hipped, in a long dress. The three women ate together, coarse rice, spinach, and kidney beans from a large round tray. Outside the compound, fenced in by a long thatch, came the sounds of men shouting, and an automobile grinding and groaning its angry way over the potholed road. A brief quick thumping of boots on the ground, from a few armed men marching past. An assorted gang of children shouting in a chorus, running along together and perhaps following the men. When the three women had eaten and washed their hands and mouths, they sat back and relaxed and chewed a weed.

The two local women chatted, their voices guttural and animated, and as Holly watched them, amused by their frank expressions, she did not feel threatened by them. At length the older woman said something to Holly, and the younger woman translated,—Come, the chief wants to meet you. They gave her army-style fatigues to put on but no underwear. She put on her boots, which mercifully the women had preserved. They all laughed.

THIRTEEN

THE SUN WAS COOL BUT BLINDING, a blustery wind blew eddies of dust on the street, the odd leaf trailing along listlessly as I emerged from the transit station. Yonge and Eglinton Square was jammed with people, throngs holding up car traffic at the crossroads. A sign high over the square flashed an ad for exclusive adventure trips to Mars and our Moon, followed immediately by another one enticing the passerby with virgin beaches inside the Long Border, with the caption, The Great Long Beach. A tower wall-screen showed news from around the world, as it happened, while a moving strip across it listed the various important indices of our collective well-being. The stock markets had taken a turn up, happiness was pink. Back on earth, in one smoky corner of the farmer's market sausages sizzled on the grill, and in the open-air restaurant next to it customers sat in a heated outdoors oblivious of the blistering cold surrounding them. I reminded myself to take some Quebec cheese home as I protected my face from the blowing dust and began to cross the square towards Lovelys Café. The pavement outside was a scene of commotion and for a moment I hesitated. A sign held up over the crowd shouted, *Die, your time is past!* Yonge and Eglinton always draws the protesters.

It's not only the young, the BabyGens, who want us oldies out of the picture so they can finally inherit the earth. It's also, for completely different reasons, the religious groups who oppose life rejuvenation. Fortunately these pro-deathers, as they call themselves, are fewer in number, though they tend to be dramatic and colourful.

Rejuve, to the monotheists, goes against the wishes of the Almighty God who planned and created the universe just so, arranging a fixed span of life for each soul therein, at the end of which He shall sit in Judgment over it. God gives life and takes it away. There is an afterlife, with a heaven and a hell. You have no right dodging His archangel of death to avoid your reckoning. He'll get you anyway. The contradictions in this position are obvious to us nonbelievers. Whether they believe that judgment comes to each soul individually and immediately after death, or there is a collective Judgment Day at the end of all life, the unspoken fear of the God-believers is that with rejuvenation the reckoning gets postponed—in principle, forever. And that won't do for the Almighty. Meanwhile some of His believers show no qualms in doing the archangel's work for him.

For the Hindus and Buddhists, rejuvenation interferes with karma and the cycle of rebirths. Imitating rebirth, constructing new lives at a whim, makes a mockery of karma and the universal law of Vishnu, Brahma, and Shiva. Why prolong life artificially when you will be reborn anyway, continuously, until by your own karma that cycle is finally broken and the self finds bliss? The purpose of life is to terminate the cycle, not prolong it.

I reached the famous display window on Yonge Street occupied by four assorted dissenters in their ongoing protest against, as they saw it, the crude scientism and life-engineering of our terrible modern Age of Kali. For more than two years these self-exhibitionists had threatened to end their lives by publicly going up in flames in this window. Did they expect the world to change then? Technology to take a step back? Human knowledge to obliterate a portion of itself? But graciously they had declared that they would not interfere with the eternal cycle—the dance of Shiva and the repose of Brahma. They would kindle themselves only at their predestined, allotted times, which—here was the catch—would be revealed to each of them privately during their meditations. Meanwhile the suspense had been mounting, the days were counted, and they were a public attraction. Three of them were of Indian origin—two bald men in saffron robes and a woman with long, loose hair in a white sari, seated silently on the floor in elegant yoga postures, beatific smiles on their smooth faces and broad white marks twitching like worms on their foreheads; the fourth one was a tall Japanese-featured man with short cropped hair wearing a white cotton kurta-shirt and pants, and he was standing, head lifted up and staring far away. His hands were joined in front of him in a pranam. Sanskrit chanting and a sonorous droning made up the soundtrack to this scene. The four had already been arrested once, then released, for obviously they had committed no crime. On the sidewalk outside the window were gathered their noisy supporters, wearing saffron or white, handing out flyers, chanting and beating on tambourines. It all looked jolly but was not a place for me to linger.

At Lovelys a few stores up, as I stepped inside the doorway, in the corner to the right I spied Presley Smith, seated back on a brown armchair, reading, his rust-red Afro prominent as a beacon in the crowded room. The armchair across from him was empty and apparently reserved for me, and having brought my order from the counter, I sank into it.

—Hello, Presley.

He looked up. So you came, Doc.

—Of course.

We sipped our drinks in silence awhile, my own coffee appropriately fortified for my generation, his, I don't know. I wondered what he was thinking as he looked away from me. The place was fairly full and noisy, customers wandered around searching for seats. Did he know the Department wanted him back—had recalled him? That would explain his elusive behaviour—the coded reply to my message, this anonymous, crowded meeting place in the city. He was afraid.

—Where have you been, Pres? We tried reaching you from the clinic. Did you get our message?

He turned towards me and smiled dimly.—Well, here I am, Doc. What can I do for you?

No longer the patient speaking to his doctor. No warmth or show of appreciation at my concern. Yet he had responded to my message, asked me to meet him. He needed me.

—Yes. How are you?

That sounded lame, and I began again:—I mean, how have you coped, Pres, with your condition?

—I'm coping.

—Good. I received a call from DIS.

He raised his eyebrows, then said drily,—The Department of Internal Security.

—Yes. The Department. Have they been in touch?

—Why would they . . .

In the ensuing silence while his glance shifted around the room, I imagined his mind working, debating how much to trust me. Finally he turned back to me.

—And what did they want?

We'd been speaking in lowered voices so as not to be overheard. Now I leaned forward and asked,—Listen, Pres, have you known that you are a DIS client? That—

—I didn't before, but now I'm not surprised . . .

He became thoughtful, then repeated,—What did they want?

—They say they are responsible for you, and they insist that they are the ones to cure your problem, which can get serious. It's nobody else's business, definitely not mine. It's they who gave you your fiction. I am to tell you that, if I see you.

—Do *you* believe it can get serious?

—Very much so. But I've advised you of that before.

A thought leads to others, begins a chain reaction until the mind cannot control that other life surging in from the past. The result is an angry storm of mental activity, a total breakdown. I had once seen such a sufferer in a professional demonstration. The patient was raving, shouting all kinds of nonsense. The condition has been called *possession,* and has been likened to the superstition of possession by a malicious bodyless entity, a spirit.

—And how did DIS know about my problem?

—We registered your data, updated your medical file, and so on. That must have raised a flag. You are their man. But it's also possible . . .

—Yes?

—I suspect that they always have an eye on their clients. What a word, *clients.*

He nodded slowly.—I carry a dark secret, then, do I? What am I then really—some schoolyard shooter? A sexual predator? A terrorist?

I said nothing, and he too turned silent, drawing a deep breath as he sat up and looked around him. When at length he began to speak, his hardness had melted a little.

—I'll be honest with you. When I left your clinic, I had a feeling I was being watched . . . I felt nervous, actually . . . and later that morning when I reached my work I received a message from something called Abdo Clinic asking me to go see them urgently. I checked—Abdo is run by DIS. I knew I had to hide—don't ask me why. Call it instinct. I decided to move in with a friend ... I'm sure the neighbours will look after Oscar. My cat.

We watched as two female supporters of the pro-death group took their teas and cakes and sat down a few tables away. Both had fresh, healthy faces, hair tightly pulled back into thick ponytails. They both wore saris.

Presley asked,—You think I should go to them?

—I think you should.

—Why?

—They know you, they are better able to cure you. And besides, they won't let anyone else touch you.

—They could turn me into someone else—again.

There was nothing to say to that. He was right, of course. If he returned to them they would no doubt toy with his memory. He would be back in the hands of the diabolical X, and there was no saying what that mind would dream up to revise Presley Smith. A new edition. But did it matter if he didn't remember his old self? No, but some people remain attached to who they are, they don't want to leave voluntarily.

I imagined that Presley would choose to remain unavailable.

—Tell me, Doc—he said and smiled, finally.—Why did you get in touch with me the way you did? Rather secretive, wasn't it? Do you usually care about your patients this much?

—I like to think so. I called you, no answer. Naturally I was concerned, knowing your condition. I felt responsible—

you had come to see me first . . . The manner in which I contacted you? Pure luck . . .

I smiled, he did likewise.

—How? he asked.

—I was on the Holly Chu site, and while scanning the messages I came across one that I thought could be from you. So I wrote my note and I'm happy it reached you.

—You knew I was on the run.

—I wasn't sure how you would respond to a call from DIS. I wanted to talk to you in private, see what you had to say for yourself.

He smiled again.

—Perhaps not luck after all.

—What, then?

He didn't reply, glanced away.

I asked him,

—Have you had any more of these thoughts—I mean, has the condition worsened? Can you control them? You said last time that you could.

—Yes.

He took a moment to reflect, looking out the window behind me; finally he leaned forward and said softly,

—Listen, Doc: *A bookstore, every wall covered with old books. A bridal veil. A cat barking.* These three intruders came knocking on my door recently. I threw them out on their ear! I'll let you know if more of them arrive.

The humour was a poor disguise.

—You should go to DIS, Pres. They can stop it.

—I'm trying some mental exercises. Yoga. If they don't

work, maybe. He got up.—I must rush, Doc. Stay in touch. See you at Chu's, perhaps.

—Contact me if you need help . . .

I watched the conspicuous fiery-topped figure weaving its way between the tables. How long could he stay in hiding? How long before he was discovered, how long before his condition overwhelmed him?

One of the sari-clad pro-deathers had come over and was looming over me, beaming goodwill and exuding a strong and sweet fragrance. I acknowledged with a gesture that the seat opposite me was now vacant and she sat down.

—Life is a cage, she said cheerfully, moving closer as she put a small stack of pamphlets on the table between us. Changing her metaphors, she continued, in a warm, rich voice,—The cycle of births chains us to the earth, from which we must seek release. I am Radha, by the way. Namaskar. I bow to you.

She joined her hands.

—I'm Frank. I bow to you too.

She giggled. She was a good-looking woman in an unconventional way, full of face, her well-developed figure shifting gracefully in her olive sari. Her neck was white, her arms deliciously plump. The large red dot on her forehead was hypnotic, like a source of her personal magnetism. She sounded quite insane.

—I'm not sure I understand you, I told her.

—Life is an illusion.

And I felt trapped at that moment, in that place. I glanced around; it all looked normal and only too real. Again she leaned forward, the red dot magnetic. I wondered, quite irrationally, as I caught a whiff of her perfume, if she sang, while she went on with her message.

—Real life is eternal, it is of the soul.

—I'm sorry, I'm not religious—

—Why delude yourself?

At my utter astonishment, she explained,—You're a rejuvie, aren't you, Frank?

—And you are one of those who believe the world would be better off without me in it. What do you want me to do, kill myself?

She laughed again with genuine delight, and I could only join her in return.

—No, that's going against karma. But you can be part of the Live Krishna movement. And you'll never be afraid of death. In fact, you will become truly immortal. No false face or artificial limbs or transplanted organs, and no false memories. The soul is beautiful and immortal, Frank, the body is . . . ugly and corruptible. It will for sure rot away, whatever you do. I would like to leave this with you—

She handed me a brightly coloured pamphlet with a picture of a chubby blue baby floating in the clouds and said,

—Come to our meetings.

I smiled my demurral and we left the café together. Outside, she beamed at me and squeezed my arm and joined the singing, tambourine-thumping demonstrators, and I kept walking, free at last from the intoxicated clutches of holiness. Why are the deluded so happy? Or is it the other way around?

———

Back in my office, I gave a curious glance at Radha's pamphlet, and before I knew it, it had drawn me in. It had five channels, three of them showing bright, colourful pictures of gods, one gave information about the Live Krishna movement in Toronto and elsewhere, and the last one displayed these lines, apparently mouthed by the blue god Krishna:

As the spirit of our mortal body wanders on
in childhood and youth and old age
the spirit wanders on to a new body:
of this the sage has no doubt

What sage? I wondered for a moment, then realized that the term in the verse referred to anyone wise enough to its truth; in that case he or she would be the sage and teacher. What a democratic thought! But was the truth of this verse so far from the truth of rejuvenation that I practised? People do wander into new bodies, in a manner of speaking, aided by surgeons and plastics and metals; and surely karmic incarnation—if that's the term—does not mean the spirit takes the old memories with itself into a new body? I should tell her this!

I pulled out my notepad and placed it before me. With some trepidation I wrote out what Presley had described for me:

A bookstore, every wall covered with old books
A bridal veil

Questions flew into my mind—where, this bookstore? I tried to imagine one, with physical books on shelves. And a bridal veil? Whose wedding? I could not recall having been to one myself. These images very evidently were from another time, like the antique car. His third fragment was eerie:

A cat barking

FOURTEEN

THE MAN FROM DIS was dressed in a grey suit, white shirt, and what looked like a school tie. He had a striking, narrow face with a deep forehead and prominent nose. His voice had none of the metal of Dauda and his manner was friendly. His name was Joe Green. He sat down across from me and began his spiel.

—Dr Sina, I am an admirer of your work—the therapy, of course, as a senior memory specialist. But more so, your academic work on the transmission of personality traits. Or is it their conservation? Your contribution has not waned over the years, and it has been extremely useful to us at the Department.

—Thank you, Joe. That's generous of you. Though I've never been told how exactly you find my work useful.

I was merely teasing. He returned my smile.

—Believe me, it's used, Doctor. And your work is proudly supported by the Department, as you know.

—Yes, and I've not failed to acknowledge that generous support in my publications and lectures.

—Of course, Doctor. We wouldn't think otherwise. And we are always grateful to be acknowledged.

I put him down for a younger GN. He did not seem in a hurry, and after a pause, during which he quickly looked around the room, he continued in the same chatty manner,

—Dr Sina. We are well aware that the Department is treated with suspicion—some wariness—by the public. That's understandable. But it's the security of the nation and our way of life that we work for, and we do our best. No one cares much for the police, but sometimes they are the only recourse when we're helpless. The same with the Department. The nation needs it. The world needs it.

By the *public* I presumed he meant me. What he was saying was that *I* was treating them with suspicion and not fully cooperating. He was here to reassure me. I put in my bit.

—It's one of our dilemmas, I guess. How to balance the collective and the individual interests.

—Exactly.

—The problem is, of course, the deep secrecy surrounding the Department; not knowing exactly what it is, what its functions are . . .

Or whether it keeps within our laws, though naturally I didn't say that. There was another momentary silence before he answered.

—It's necessary. Now Dr Sina, about this patient of yours—

—Presley Smith.

—He should be in our hands, as you've been informed.

—Yes, I was informed by Dauda. Tell me, is Dauda a real person?

Joe gave a chuckle.—She's our intelligent interface. They hate to be called virtual, by the way. I'll add a little secret: she has several personalities, with corresponding voices and names. She can even do Hindi and Arabic!

—Male and female?

—Male and female. He grinned.

—I'm not treating Presley anymore, Joe. He told me he could control his condition—I have no problem with that. But I was made to understand by Dauda that you'd been searching for him—I expect you've not found him?

—No, he's still at large, evading our attempts to find him. He's on the run—though why should he be? He'll be found eventually—but the sooner the better. He is a threat to himself, as you understand.

—And to the public good—or why would you be interested?

—He's our responsibility, Dr Sina. We're not so unfeeling, we do take care of our own creations.

—Why not let *me* treat him, Joe? If he returns to me, I mean. I can take him off your hands, he trusts me. Why is the Department so worked up about the condition of one man? Your interface Dauda spoke to me twice—and she sounded menacing. Now here you are.

Joe Green replied, gravely,—All right. I'll be frank—pardon the pun—and this is not to be revealed in any manner whatsoever. We are dealing with a matter of national security here, not just any public good—you will understand, Dr Sina. Presley's previous life contains details that are too sensitive and should not come out—and they will not do him any good either.

I opened my mouth to respond but he raised a hand:

—I know. Records of past lives are supposed to be destroyed. But not in special cases, you understand. Or we can't do our job effectively.

—You mean DIS preserves records.

—In some important cases, yes.

—What details from Presley's previous life . . .

There was no point in asking further. I had known of DIS's mandate to take persons who are deemed threats to our national security and render them harmless. It is one of those measures that the public would rather not discuss or acknowledge. The cities are safer, whatever it takes.

—I'm afraid I can't tell you any more, Doctor. Has he tried to contact you since his last visit?

—No, he hasn't.

Perhaps spoken too quickly, and Joe's head jerked up ever so slightly as a result. There came a slight change in his tone.

—You understand that the law requires you to cooperate fully with the Department.

—Absolutely. I understand. Of course.

—Do you think he's had other intrusions—those random thoughts—Doctor, running around in that brain of his? The lion and the red car, the baby, what next? What have you made of these strands?

He had accessed my records. Hardly unusual, it is what we expect DIS to do and we don't want to be reminded of it; it was rather the casual display of power here and now that was suddenly so disconcerting. To be reminded that you are nobody special, just one entity among a faceless public that is the often invoked nation, to whose collective demands you must submit. Any privacy you possess is a privilege that can be casually and briskly withdrawn.

Joe Green caught my look but didn't flinch. His entire approach, all the charm and deference, had the strength of authority behind it, and the potential to alter or turn off at any moment. He'd not even told me the purpose of his visit, though the threat it contained was evident. Inside those loose features hid a hard man. Dauda was all voice.

I told him,—The last time he came here he said that these thoughts which had been plaguing him were under control. The lion, and so on. He could evade them, or push them back. The accompanying depression and racing heartbeat were gone too. He was using some mind exercises— yoga, counting numbers, and so on—to help him. He wasn't in need of a treatment any longer. He was confident.

—He's not the best judge of that, as we both know. What do you think they mean—the lion, etc.? Sorry to pester you, Doctor, but you are the expert. Perhaps you should come work for us! What is the lion, if you were to venture a guess?

—The lion could symbolize a king—it does in many cultures, including ours. Real, or from a national myth, or a children's story, who knows—the lion and the unicorn and so on. And if you go back far enough, perhaps the lion represents a primal human fear of the predator. Or it could be a private code. Maybe Presley was a zookeeper in his previous life.

That last bit was a joke, and I delivered it with a smile, but Joe Green was not impressed. He looked disappointed. He stood up, shook hands.

—Thank you, Dr Sina. I appreciate your time. Don't hesitate to call me if you hear from him.

—You're welcome. I will.

—Well. Goodbye. And with a quick nod he hurried on his way out. At the door, however, like a vintage detective he turned around and fired off one final question:

—Dr Sina, what do you think of these Karmics? I couldn't help seeing that pamphlet on your desk.

—They are entitled to their beliefs. As long as they don't push us older people in front of trains.

He laughed.—Yes, but they can be dangerous. Beware of them. Well, goodbye and thanks again, Doctor.

Shortly after Joe Green's departure, Lamar knocked and beckoned me from the door. There was a wide grin on his face.

—Come and have a look here, Doc.

I followed him outside, but there seemed nothing unusual there. The phone rang and the call was answered at the control desk nearby. I turned to Lamar.

—What's the matter, Lamar?

—Look around—see anything unusual, Doc?

I didn't, but before I could respond with irritation, he took a step sideways and flung a hand behind, towards the partition.

I stepped back.—What?

Lamar gave a chuckle.—I knew you'd say that! Rather mod, wouldn't you say?

The calming northern landscape that used to adorn the light grey softboard was gone, and in its place was an equally large abstract reproduction. It was the famous Warhol, with Presley's namesake, the twentieth-century icon, reproduced several times over in cowboy gear. Hardly mod. I would have noticed it instantly if I had not been staring at a grinning Lamar. What now? The Elvises would point their guns at us all the time as we went about our work; they would point at me as I sat at my desk if the door were left open. And if it was closed, I'd still know that they were there, waiting to ambush me.

There had been talk of new wall decorations for the clinic, but no decision had been taken that I knew.

—Who ordered it? I asked Lamar.

—Dr Otieno. He said you'd like it—he knows about your patient—everybody does, he's so conspicuous. Anyway, it's on approval. Don't you like it? We all do, so far . . .

I knew that Otieno wasn't likely to spare a thought for me. This was no coincidence, or an office joke. He could only have been instructed. There must be a monitor inside the reproduction—an eye, many eyes, watching. And you could not now sneeze on the premises, let alone scratch yourself somewhere private, without being watched by Elvis.

The rest of my afternoon was free, and I decided to go home.

As I emerged from our building, a tan and sinewy-looking man of medium height, sportily dressed in jeans, a light blue jacket, and a black baseball cap, and leaning against the concourse railing, seemed to decide suddenly to straighten up and start walking too. He stayed behind me to my right. On my way I paused to meditate upon the river, as I often did. The man was on my left, looking somewhat uncomfortable and hardly engrossed by the river. Soon I continued on, and a few minutes later stopped at the flower vendor, who'd been waiting in anticipation of my custom. When I looked around this time I saw that the guy had disappeared. That I was being monitored was not very surprising; but to be tailed by a physical monitor, as though I were a common criminal in an old detective yarn?

Why did I deserve this close attention? Obviously, despite my friendly exchange with Joe Green—or perhaps because of it—the DIS believed either that I knew where Presley was or that he would soon get in touch with me— and quite rightly they didn't trust me to inform them. On the other hand, if I thought he was dangerous, I would have told them what I knew, even if that meant admitting to a deception or two. I'd already advised him to seek the Department's help. But I also believed strongly that he deserved the privacy and dignity to try and solve his problem—or at least to attend to it. He didn't deserve to be arbitrarily kidnapped and—as he put it—turned into yet someone else without his consent.

FIFTEEN

IT WAS A BRIGHT, WARM EVENING, and when I reached home we decided to have a barbecue in the backyard. The setting sun glimmered through the foliage, the river in the distance looked placid and grey. And Joanie looked beautifully composed, clutching a drink after her shower, face aglow, midriff exposed above the light blue cords that are the rage this fall, a black sweater tied around her shoulders. She is practically a carnivore, eats as much meat as she can, despite the health warnings against trace radioactive buildup in the higher levels of the food chain. I prefer what's good for my digestion, grains and greens, which she always scoffs at, saying I need meat more than she does, and it could do me less harm—meaning, I guess, that I had less at stake. And so, considerate lovers, we compromised: I ate more meat than I wished to, and she a little less. This was our world at its calmest and most blissful.

But on her tablet we now watched reports of the most recent overseas outrage. The headline banner practically shouted, in garish black letters: *HORROR INSIDE THE BORDER!* In Maskinia a busload of tourists had been waylaid and kidnapped by a militia. This had happened earlier in the afternoon and the news kept rolling in. There were pictures of the captured men and women, interviews with friends and relatives, recordings of the frightened calls some of them managed to make before their phones were taken away. There were the expected angry condemnations by the president and the prime minister, who promised to use all means possible to retrieve the hostages. Will you go to war? asked a reporter. All options are on the table, replied the president, saying in effect nothing. Their political opponents on the other hand were howling for blood.

As the night fell, we lingered together outside, despite the growing chill, she stretched out on the lounge chair and I on the blanket on the ground beside her, the partly bare tree branches rustling overhead, the sky a clear black and the first stars in focus. Once more we soberly repeated the mantra, thanked our good fortune that we lived in the civilized part of the globe, the best in every way, and we wondered aloud why anyone from these parts would wish to visit those dangerous places, stopping short of saying, Serves those tourists right for their folly and arrogance. But then I was reminded of my own visit to Maskinia as a student. A lark in March was how it was billed, that carefree getaway under a warm sun by a beach, where we were spoilt by luxury and excess. And then the reverse side to the heavenly—the shock and guilt of seeing raw deprivation, humanity degraded. The resentment, contempt, envy we saw in the locals during our sojourn into a village.

—Friendly looks too? she asked, just to test me.

—I suppose. Yes. But we felt vulnerable and scared. Even when we stopped and treated the kids to colas—which were not supposed to be safe but we all had them too—and they rushed at us happily, hands outstretched . . . That was youthful indulgence, and a long time ago. But we grew up and cured ourselves of our guilt and confused sentimentality.

The ensuing silence drew us into our own thoughts. Mine drifted towards Presley and Joe Green. The Department demanded. What had I got myself into? I thought of Radha. Rather charming, and how she had squeezed my arm. Beware of them, Joe Green had warned. Beside me Joanie stirred, and I became aware that we were being watched. From the hedge out front came a steady chorus of the night insects; in the distance somewhere down the road a girl shouted at a guy—students most likely; someone was listening to orchestra music. A figure passed beyond the hedge in the dark, and soon after a car door opened, then closed, and the car drove away. Was that my stalker?

She turned to me.—Do we have a responsibility towards them? Those people there, on the other side?

She had now put on her sweater, for it had turned decidedly chilly. Rushed by a tender feeling, I reached out and caressed the curve of her hip, mathematically smooth.

It deserved an equation with exponentials. She put her hand on mine. It felt cool.

—Yes, Joanie, I answered,—but from a distance. We must preserve our well-being now or we'll destroy human life on the planet—and everywhere else. All the culture and civilization, the civic and social fabric of our existence—a wonderful, complex construct that actually functions. Think about it . . . we've come to it after centuries of experience, history . . . much of it violent . . .

My voice almost cracked at this, and she gave me a quick look. Where did that emotion come from? I believed what I'd just said but had never articulated it this way, and so strongly, as though—now I think about it—I sensed also the tip of a reservation and had to push it back. If we allow doubts about ourselves, then where are we?

We became silent and perhaps she was thinking about what I had just said. Then she observed,

—This complex construct surely includes charity; surely it includes our relationship with them; surely we're a part of them as they are of us.

—Of course. But a diseased part, then. An incurable part.

—I don't agree.

Later, inside the house, this intimacy extended into lovemaking, and as I lay back I marvelled at my willpowered performance—lowering myself from the lofty philosophical to the precarious male animal. Perhaps it was the tension of the last few days that was the aphrodisiac.

Why did my sexual performance so obsess me? Because it affirmed my new, rejuvenated life? My worth as her partner?

I was intrigued and unsettled by her line of questioning. I would never have imagined her capable of paying heed to, let alone showing compassion for, those out there who are commonly dismissed as the Barbarians. If she had expressed any serious thought before, I had not paid attention. The young to me were beautiful, selfish, and narcissistic. Perhaps I had got off on the wrong tack with her, seeing all along only her physical flawlessness and good nature to my repaired decrepitude and anxieties. I should have thought of her as a partner and equal in every way. Instead, I'd patronized and babied her all along. I was the narcissist, obsessed with myself.

But then why blame myself only? Shouldn't she have imposed otherwise on me than she did? Did my age—my oldness—intimidate her? She had patronized me in return.

When she was asleep and beautifully sonorous, I gave her a peck on the tip of her nose and padded over to the study.

SIXTEEN

The Notebook

Holly Chu, you've been inside my skin as Presley has. I sit here and evoke you, why I cannot explain. Forgive me if I misrepresent you in this alternative reality that I create—speculate?—for you. And for me. I could not imagine you dead and eaten, that there was not some humanity in those people there jostling against the brutality. How can we believe only the worst of them when there are children also running around laughing and playing, and men and women do occasionally sing and love? You showed them to us. We didn't see. I refused to see. Except here.

Joanie: Surely we are a part of them as they are of us . . . I should have listened to you, Joanie, and then perhaps I could have kept you away from the clutches of the Friend.

#48

The Journalist

Layela, the woman who had become her lover, took her outside and down the street, along which Holly had strolled
innocently only the day before, in her Safari Apparel outfit,
her little mike on her collar to collect all the sounds for her
audience back home. The street was noisy and crowded as
usual, a few small trucks were parked at the side. People
looked at her but not more curiously than before—foreign-
ers did strange things anyway. Making small talk as they
walked, they went past a small mosque, a boxlike building, from which began a faint, half-hearted prayer call,
and across a littered unbuilt lot on to the next street, which
looked similar to the first but was quieter, and closed off
halfway by a towering wooden gate some twenty feet high.
Three young men stood guard, automatics slung casually
round their shoulders. Making sly, suggestive comments,
they opened a squeaky door within the gate to let the two
women enter an enclosed settlement. The road they were
on branched into two short streets that curved and met
further ahead. The houses here were of faded white stone,
as in Layela's street, but better preserved if smaller. The two
women took the rightmost and larger and busier of the roads
and passed a few women sitting outside their houses, busy
with domestic chores, children playing around them. There
came sounds of television and music from the surroundings
and, when she paid more attention, the vaporous aroma of

cooked rice, and the very typical clamour of older kids at a school somewhere. A customer stood outside a supply shop, chatting with the stall owner; further up there appeared to be a garage, from which a jeep reversed and then turned and came in their direction and passed them. The two walking women merited barely a glance. If not for the sight of the occasional weapon on the men, the scene looked tranquil. Suddenly they were beside a long wall on their right, recently painted white, with a blue border at the bottom. Stark as the weapons on the street was the steel barbed wire that topped this wall. At its centre was an opening with a gate, through which the two women entered into a compound. It was paved smoothly with cement and partly covered with a mat, and furnished with assorted chairs and a low table. The walls were hung with brightly coloured cloth, gashes of yellow, brown, black, and green. In the middle of this compound, on an antique wooden chair with a high straight back, sat a distinguished-looking elder with a flowing white beard and long hair, wearing a black robe embroidered with a green thread. His skin was the colour of polished oak, his eyes were deep brown. His mouth had a thin half-smile upon it. His arms rested on the flat, wide armrests of his chair, his curved right forefinger steadily and very lightly beating on it. He wore brown beads around his neck.

Layela went forward, bowed to the elder, and kissed his hand. She turned to Holly and said,—Greet Nkosi, our chief and protector.

Holly stepped forward to do as bid.

SEVENTEEN

—HI, SAID RADHA.—Fancy seeing you again.

—You mean you never expected to see me ever again?

She smiled. It's karma.

This time, failing to get one of the sofas, I'd found myself a high perch at the window of Lovelys, overlooking Yonge Street. It was windy outside, dust blowing, people in a hurry. A few wisps of her brown hair had run loose down the side of her face. She'd just walked in.

—May I, she said and took the next stool.

She quickly tidied up her hair and swept an imagined fleck of dust from one cheek. The red dot on her forehead was as bewitching as before.

I had returned to Lovelys hoping I'd find her here. Being silly, I told myself, but there'd been something attractive and positive about her last time that I found catching. I'd never met anyone so straightforward and forthcoming. Trusting. Happy. Sunny. Her thoughts about life intrigued me too, even though I didn't believe any of them.

Perhaps she'd guessed that I'd returned only to see her, for she inched closer. And the sari, I noticed, was very cling-ing and sensual. She noticed my naughty stare.

—What a coincidence! Do you work nearby? What kind of work do you do, Frank?

—I'm a doctor . . .

—A doctor! What kind?

—Just an ordinary one.

What kind of doctor doesn't like to say? My kind. Would she understand if I told her I gave people new memories so they could begin new lives? No. She didn't believe in break-ing the karmic cycle. Well, if it's breakable, why not?

—And you? I asked.—What line of work are *you* in?

—I'm a people facilitator—a friend-maker. I help people make friends.

What did that mean, I wondered. A matchmaker of sorts? The attendant announced my drink and cheerfully placed it before me in a large mug. He shouted loudly enough for all to find out that here was a special coffee fortified to help the aged keep young. But I was not the only one there who'd ordered it.

—Be my friend, then.

—I *am* your friend.

—Oh. And I guess I'm yours.

—You must be *certain*. I know you are. Are you still assessing me?

And we stared at each other, our smiles not of seductive parrying but of friendly jousting.

I asked,—Do you come here every day, to protest? That's hard work.

—Except weekends. I see you don't think much of what we do.

—I don't see the point, to be honest. Do you expect to change the world? Do you think people will give up their chance to live longer? It doesn't seem to me that way. Progress proceeds one way—forward.

I pointed with a finger for emphasis. Mischievously, she grabbed it with one hand, then let it go.

—I see you're going to be a hard case.

—You want to change the world.

—Yes. And today I'll start with you. I'll be honest with you too. I know what you do. Someone pointed you out to me once, on the street. You are a well-known doctor. A *rejuvie* doctor.

—It's not that I operate a concentration camp.

She laughed delightedly.—Don't be so serious. I didn't mean it that way. But you see, you, most people, are under the illusion that natural life ends and must therefore be lengthened artificially. Well, I've got news for you. It doesn't. The body ends. The soul returns in another body. And I've got more news for you. There is an eternal life which is even better than this one . . .

And thus she went on. I was tempted to tease her, Then what would be the point of your pamphlet with the blue child-god and the chanting and singing? How does that garish display accommodate the idea of eternal life and the soul? I knew she would have to resort to that cure-all of symbolism, but not wanting to spoil the mood, I kept quiet and just watched her. There was perhaps a silly smile on my face, such was her charm. Simply listening to her speak was enjoyable—the impassioned voice, the friendly manner not yielding even for a moment.

I was not unaware that it was her naïve beliefs that rendered the woman before me so deliriously happy; they left no room for irony and cold reason. The curse of so many of us. She was blessed. We spent more time together than her customary tea break, and I'd not enjoyed myself so much for a long time and felt as free of anxiety. When we got up, we agreed to meet again at the same place next week.

On the train back I allowed a feeling of guilt at my faithlessness. I had no excuse, not even that I was repaying Joanie in kind. I'd done what I was not expected to do, I'd acted out of character—and it had brought about a quiet sort of happiness in me, an understated exhilaration. Surely that was bad faith. Joanie did what she did, without stealth, without much joy either. I knew that. I was the anchor in her life, the support of our relationship. Did I have a right to be happy on my own? In secret? I was the cursed one.

———

Back at the clinic, I completed some reports and took a phone call from DNI, the Department of New Identities, regarding Sheila Walktall, and gave the bureaucrat my opinion on her application. He said would I reconsider? Her physician had strongly recommended she be allowed to go ahead with a transition. Her personal problems merited that. I agreed to see her again. It was a little later than usual when I left. On my way out, Lamar approached me, grinning, and explained to me the cause of the hubbub in the outer office some moments ago.

—Did you hear, Doc? Holly is alive!—that reporter who was eaten!

After making suitable exclamations, and having laughed at a joke about how Holly might have tasted, I hurried home, rather rattled. I could not quite rationalize to myself why I felt the way I did—not happy. On my way I thought I heard a cry or two of *Holly's alive!* Someone said *Traitor!*—the significance of which I would only realize later.

What's happened to you, Holly Chu? You're alive, after all . . . and turned into one of *them*? You were better off dead, our girl hero. But who am I to say that.

Is someone playing a joke?

There was a brazen new image on her Profile. A thin smile on her face, wearing army fatigues, she was standing on a dirt road holding a red flag in one hand and a raised automatic weapon in the other. She hadn't looked very strong before, that gun she was holding up could not be light.

There was a young dark woman with her, slim and tall, standing behind and to a side. It was a posed photo, with a patchy green landscape and a blue sky in the background, both girls looking wide-eyed at the camera. Holly looked drained and pale, her hair was uncombed, but there was a definite glow on the other one's face.

A boldfaced banner under the two women proclaimed: *BRING THE BORDER DOWN! WE ARE NOT RATS! OWEO!—ONE WORLD FOR EVERY ONE!*

No, this was no joke. She was alive, and that picture, as we know, would soon find itself on a radical poster. All those messages of sympathy, the heap of bouquets on her Profile, had been replaced by vicious invective. *You bitch, you communist Asian cunt, you traitor* . . . Heaps of shit. Overnight, Holly became the most hated creature this side of the Long Border.

Who was the real Holly Chu? The curious, good-natured, and well-meaning Toronto girl who loved to report from faraway places, or the revolutionary behind the Border? *We're a part of them as they are of us . . .*

We who have violated personal history and personal relationships in our bid to become immortal, can we now really know for certain who we are?

EIGHTEEN

—OKAY, OKAY, I GRANT YOU THIS—Bill Goode, wearing an off-white collarless Indian jacket over a blue shirt to match his hair, was saying to his guest, both now seated on easy chairs behind a low, long table, Bill holding up a hand to surrender the point.—They don't actually *eat* people—but they Chu'd this one up proper!

He turned his head to flash his wide smile at the audience, who broke out into predictable laughter. There were shouts of approval. A delayed guffaw was followed by more laughter.

The guest was Ralph Bloom, a middle-aged academic in a grey suit and red tie.

Bill asked him,—And you call it what, the Finland syndrome?

—Stockholm. The Stockholm syndrome, Ralph responded patiently, knowing full well that the error was deliberate.

—In which the victim, one Holly Chu of XBN, spouts the cause of her victimizers. Actually demands ransom for the kidnapped tourists! Can you believe this! Come on, Ralph. Here's one of our best and brightest, from a good and accomplished family and educated at one of our best universities at great expense—and known personally to me and liked and supported by all of us here at the station—what's going on? We've been *bazoonked!*

—In the Stockholm syndrome, said Ralph,—for which there are numerous precedents, the victim is frightened and confused, and in that state, a part of her mind empathizes with her kidnappers' cause—which in a simplistic way seems to make sense to her—to many of us, in fact. Subconsciously the victim at the same time believes that by pleasing her kidnappers she can win her freedom. She's wrong, for her victimizers are terrorists and cowards.

—It doesn't look like a *part* of her mind that's doing the talking. Look, she's holding up a gun and she's the one making the demands. And let me tell you, she's convincing and scary. It's Dr Jekyll and Ms Hyde. She believes what she's saying. Don't tell me she doesn't!

A shaky, blurry image of Holly Chu dropped down in front of Bill and Ralph, and spoke to the audience. It had been transmitted from Maskinia.

—*I am Umoja wa Kwanza of the Freedom Warriors of Maskinia. We have taken nineteen of your overfed, ignorant citizens as hostages. Peeping Tom tourists such as these come to gawk while our people die of hunger, disease, and radiation . . .*

Her North Atlantic accent and her clean features, despite the oversize fatigues, seemed to belie her message but made its threat more real and believable. If this could happen to one of us, if a privileged young woman, known and admired, suddenly joined the terrorists, anything was possible.

—For the release of these nineteen hostages we demand five hundred million dollars, half in small WCUs, the remainder as gold. Further instructions will be forthcoming when our demands are agreed upon. Failure to agree will result in dire consequences for these Peeping Tom tourists.

On the set, Bill Goode exploded with derision.

—Umo—Umo-de-kwango—what kind of name is that?

He turned to his audience, and the hall filled up with hilarity that, however, quickly abated as Ralph Bloom spoke up to be heard.

—Umoja wa Kwanza. It means Unity First. The Freedom Warriors is a well-known militia, in fact, that has periodically transformed itself—and re-emerged under different names. It's died only to revive again.

—Like those insect species you find there in those hot climes . . . uuurrrgh!

Bill Goode gave an exaggerated shudder, moving his hands and fingers in the air in a simulation of a crawling insect, and again the laughter predictably broke out. Ralph Bloom, an expert on *there,* gave a strained smile.

Bill straightened up like a naughty boy, put on a serious face, and asked,—D'you think we'll pay this outrageous ransom?

—I'm sure that negotiations are taking place. The key to resolving such crises is always secrecy and time bought.

—Well, we should send the troops in and crush them once again, Bill Goode announced, making a squeezing gesture with his thumb, then placing both hands on the table in front of him and throwing a puppy look at the audience. He was rewarded again with extended applause.

A sense of disbelief lay heavy upon the media, stunned by the knowledge that the air had suddenly gone out of its headline story: *they* turned out not to be cannibals, one of us actually turned into them, rejecting our civilization and values, which we justly celebrate. This was the new headline story.

Holly Chu's Profile showed a new main image. She appeared in fatigues and a beret, sitting outdoors behind a table with her weapon resting by her hand. The caption underneath said: Umoja wa Kwanza Freedom Warrior. There was no music. A paragraph of biographical information explained Holly's conversion.

She was born in Denver, granddaughter of an African woman and a Chinese railway worker sent to Africa on an assistance program in the twentieth century. Ever since her school days in Denver she had been disturbed by the disparity in the lifestyles and wealth on the two sides of the Border. It was obscene and a crime. (I have suppressed the exclamations.) On the other side, people lived in abject conditions, fearful for their lives, without governments to protect them; they were exposed to nuclear radiation, subjected to rape and brutalized by the militias, and dependent on food and water dropped as aid from the sky—the portion that was not stolen; on our side, especially the North Atlantic, people lived in clean and safe cities, ate healthy food, had time for leisure, and were already extending their lives into the third generation. On her travels in Maskinia, Bimaru, and other places as a reporter for XBN, she was shocked by the horror and hopelessness she witnessed. Many a night she had wept in frustration after hearing stories of people's suffering. When she was in Toronto she had begun sending money to charities. But she had soon realized that this was simply patronizing. What did it take for the rich to throw away loose change to the poor? They felt good about themselves while the poor continued to live in perpetual humiliation. There was needed a complete change in the world order. Revolution. You could not wait for things to change by themselves. You have to grab the initiative, take the first step. So now in Maskinia she had decided to join the Freedom Warriors and do something about it. She exhorted young people in the privileged world to also take action in support of those on the other side of the Border.

And do what? I muttered to myself. The world is not going to change, you're smart enough to know that. There will always be the poor. Frustration. Desperation. Then madness if you tempt it. Ralph Bloom was right. Holly's was a delusion brought on by the shock of her capture.

In her mailbox, while perusing the messages, most of them filled with hatred and a few, surprisingly, with bravos, I came across an angry diatribe embedded with this one line: *And Frenchie, it's threatening to flood and I am at my wits' end. Leo the Cat.* It was Presley, of course, and the *nom de plume* brought on a smile that lived but an instant. The message was far from humorous and hidden cleverly enough, though a wary Cyliton could possibly catch it. It was a distress call.

I did not know what to do. Presley had said he'd moved in with a friend, but how to find him? Using the phone was risky. Could there be a clue in his Sunflower record? But he no longer existed there, as I quickly found out now.

TOM: *Can I assist you, Frank? You appear to be stumped.*

FRANK: *I am. Why is my patient Presley Smith not in the records? We registered him at the Sunflower, I know that. Can you find him?*

TOM: *If he's been deliberately removed, Frank, it would not be worthwhile to try and trace him further.*

FRANK: *Why? Surely you can help me. It's urgent that I find him. I have a message for him.*

TOM: *Sorry, Frank. I need an authorization, Frank. Then I can help you.*

It was more than likely that my inquiry was flagged the moment I started searching—though I had the ready explanation that I was only attempting to help them find Presley.

I confirmed that Presley's Public Profile had also been pulled. It was as though he had never been. They had created him, in some sense, published him, as they themselves put it, and now like some banned or dangerous book they had withdrawn him. If he didn't receive help soon, I knew that he would suffer terribly.

No probes into my brain, Doc, he'd said. They could turn him into someone else again.

Had he chosen collapse and death to that terrible alternative? Did he have any idea of the past that DIS was so desperate to suppress?

NINETEEN

THE NEWS WAS EVERYWHERE: the following day at precisely a minute past noon, one of the Karmic Four, on self-
display at the store window on Yonge Street at Eglinton
Avenue, set himself on fire in full view of supporters and
voyeurs. For the moment, for one afternoon and evening to
be precise, Holly Chu and the kidnap victims in Maskinia
were sidelined, and Virendra Kumar, professor of religion
at Trinity College, was splashed upon screens and projected
in media rooms as he went ablaze and turned to smoke and
ash. The professor had ended his life on earth, confident of
return in another and better life or, even better still, of complete liberation from the physical world. His press release
said he was a proud G0 and forty-six.

In the suicide scene that was broadcast, the four protesters are situated inside the brightly lit window just as I had seen them last—two men in saffron robes and a woman in white sari seated serenely around a central image of Shiva (as I've learned to recognize the god), perfectly composed in a yoga posture. The fourth, the Japanese man in white pyjamas and long shirt, is standing and staring straight ahead—engaging infinitude, one presumes, or nothing. Droning from an Indian string fills the soundtrack. Grey spirals of incense smoke waft up from one corner. All of a sudden one of the sitting men springs up onto his feet with an incomprehensible throaty utterance, then bounds towards an earthen pot lying on a stool, picks it up, and pours from it a clear fluid upon his head and body. He flashes out a lighter from somewhere within his clothes and with a flick sets himself aflame. The saffron robe is consumed in an instant. The two seated fellow protesters stare passively before them, the standing one keeps staring at infinity. The observers on the sidewalk are dumbfounded, there are screams, as the burning man—the muscle and bone turning red then black, the hair burning up, head ghostly and teeth gleaming—stands still, then collapses in a heap of ashen residue without uttering a sound. Fire engines, police vehicles, and two ambulances arrive noisily outside. The scene is not for the queasy.

The professor left behind a wife, Lata, and two boys. In an interview recorded at the site, Lata, looking wasted, told the reporters in a toneless voice,—No, he has not died. Only his body has died.

———

—You watched him die, I said to Radha, my tone accusing. I did not actually see her in the news reports but presumed she had been on the scene.

Taken aback, she opened her mouth to protest:

—But I was on the other side of the window, on the street, and there were *dozens* of people in front of me!—what *could* I have done? When I found out what had happened, he was already dead . . .

Her voice fell, and she looked expectantly at me, for a sign of understanding, perhaps.

—Would you have stopped him, if you could?

She took a moment, then shook her head and said, softly,—No.

Her hands fell together on her lap, and a strand of hair slipped to the edge of her eye. Her face was moist. The room was hot.

Death—needless death—is an utter waste. There are times when death is unavoidable, of course—when a brain cannot be revived, or a useless, broken body is beyond repair. To me life is contained energy that by its nature and definition resists extinction, has a will to survive. It was my job to help it go on living, to extend the ability for a consciousness to continue to reside within a body and experience itself and the world outside. And so, needless death, a wilful extinction of this energy, such as Professor Kumar's self-immolation, is like destroying a diamond by pulverizing it.

I was drawn that morning to come see the scene of the suicide, repelled as I was by the thought of it. Call it research. People had stopped to gawk and protesters were still active and loud next door outside the display window, which though empty was guarded by police. The remaining three Karmic protesters of the shop window were in custody, as was the shop owner. The shop was closed.

Of course, I had hoped to find Radha at Lovelys—even though this was not the day we had fixed to meet. She was seated on a sofa, had kept the other one reserved.

—For me? I asked.

She nodded.—I knew you'd come.

It was a good thing too, for the café was more crowded than usual. I had also hoped I might find Presley here. A desperate hope, I knew, for would he be in a condition to commute? Was it even safe for him to be seen?

Radha hadn't seen him again either.

—Who is he? A patient of yours? Don't you have his contact?

—He's a patient, yes, but I've lost his contact. He's someone whose past life keeps returning to plague his mind. It can kill him. I must find him.

She said nothing, looked somewhat discomfited. Something told her that this was privileged information. Then she offered,—Yogis who are advanced in their meditations have been known to recall their past lives. With concentration you can do that.

—Can you? What were you in your past life?

—I'm not advanced—and that's not funny.

Her lips pursed, she was offended and hurt. So that she wouldn't get up and go away, I hastened to apologize.

—I'm sorry—I wasn't joking—well, not completely . . . But in our case, what *we* deal with is a brain thing. We can control these recollections in the clinic. And in any case what's a previous life nowadays? We can even manufacture a patient's past.

She gave me a stiff stare, then said sternly, with a quick shake of her head,—I think people like you have confused our existence, you have lost the point and meaning of life. There *is* a previous life—it belongs to the soul. The soul is eternal. It goes from body to body in the cycle of births. It transmigrates. It collects the impressions of our actions— that is the basis of morality. Or don't you believe in morality? Only when the soul becomes clean of this karma does it become free. That freedom is the point of life.

What could I say to that? She saw disbelief, agnosticism on my face, and said, almost sulkily,—Tell me: what happens when someone really dies—is burnt to death, for example. Or when a baby is born. What then?

—Nothing, really. All we do—I do—is help people to cope with their unwanted memories. Many people reach a stage when they want simply to quit—families, relationships, disappointments—and start afresh. Especially when they've got along in years and there's a lot of baggage from the past . . . which they would rather shed off and begin new lives. So we give them new identities, new lives with new memories, and they renew themselves in mind and body. It's simple, and it's what people want. They have a right to live as long as they can, to be as happy as possible.

She looked pleased that I had troubled myself to make my case.

—And those who can't afford such procedures, they just die? It's a luxury for the rich that you're describing. And what about the young, as the old proliferate and take over the world?

She looked—beautiful? No, sensual, in that combative state. Instinctively I grabbed her hand across the table. It was soft and warm. Our eyes locked, hers large and black, in between them that red dot. She was in her early forties, I surmised. And there you go again, Frank, lusting after young flesh . . .

—Can I see you again? Here?

She nodded.

I knew nothing about her; she was just someone I flirted with at the coffee shop, but with whom I felt inordinately happy. I sent her my card, accepted hers.

—If you see my friend, tell him I was looking for him. His name is Presley.

She nodded again.

Just as we stood up, there was a loud shattering of glass and the café was filled with shouts and screams. A brick had come crashing through the front window, and an arctic blast followed in its wake. Outside, Yonge Street was in a turmoil. Radha and I went out together, in the midst of a crush of people, holding hands to stay together. We pushed our way slowly around a tight police cordon, at the same time inquiring as to what was happening. In between heads and shoulders we saw several small fires raging in the middle of the square; with spectators watching from behind the cordon, it was as though a street theatre were in progress. It took a while for us to realize that the fires on the square were effigies set ablaze to imitate the immolation of Dr Kumar.

How this show of support for the professor was not actually a mockery was not quite clear to me, but it was the young and unemployed out on a rampage once more, demanding jobs and social security. The row of blazing effigies served as a barricade in a faceoff between the rioters and police in protective gear. One of the fires was being put out. Missiles flew but not with conviction; the chanting was vociferous, the flashing signs cruelly unambiguous in their message. *LET THEM GO! THE EARTH FOR THE YOUNG! LET THE FOGEYS DIE!*

An angry young woman stepped out from among the rioters to shout her message in the face of the cops, gesturing with one arm raised above her head. It took a moment before her true significance registered. I stared long at her, in utter disbelief, my heart sinking, my throat constricting. A striking blonde, her face glowing in the firelight, her short hair as though itself aflame and fanned by the wind; her shoes red and so painfully familiar. *Joanie?*

Radha and I exchanged a look, said goodbye, and I headed off for the transit station, wondering if she too was going to join the protest. As I crossed the street some distance from the rioting, I noticed that my shadow was faithfully with me, the man wearing a baseball cap and not bothered at all to remain anonymous. I was almost comforted.

But I was glad Presley had not been at Lovelys.

It was hard to accept, the sight of Joanie in a mob demanding that people like me, and therefore I, should go away and die. But I couldn't believe either that she would hold that thought, this woman who would lean on my arm, her head on my shoulder, or make love with me, or nuzzle against me as she slept with that gentle musical snore . . . even though she was unfaithful to me. It was not personal, I told myself, it was a principle she was stating. With such passion? In her own way she loved me, I knew that. I had faith in our humanity, her decency. Her honesty. Which is not to deny that among the young protesters there would be those who would have no qualms knifing you in the gut or zapping you with those thingies they use to mug and otherwise harass older GNs. The principle is that the old make way for the young and gracefully let go. But that's not natural anymore, it goes against the face of human development and progress. Should we not do what is possible to stay alive? That's basic instinct. Didn't we in previous centuries do everything we could to protect life and prolong it? Didn't we do everything we could in the past, spend great expense and resources even against the face of reason, to keep alive the most hopeless cases? Should we kill the older folks now because progress allows them to enjoy life and live even longer instead of spending decades on sickbeds?

———

When I arrived at the clinic I noticed that I'd lost my shadow. I waited for him awhile, then went up to my office, where Elvis-Warhol, I presumed, duly registered me. More pleasing was the sight of Lamar. He is from the island of Trinidad. In the years I have known him his skin has turned progressively fairer, and his hair is dyed light brown; he looks remarkably different from his brother, and we sometimes joked about it.

I told him to come to my office, and while giving him instructions about the rest of the day, managed to murmur,

—Lamar, I've lost my shadow. They must have planted something on me.

He took my jacket to hang and went away.

My experience of the morning had left me shell-shocked. I couldn't control my thoughts. I had a headache and a depressed feeling, to alleviate which I took an extra-strength pill. I drank two glasses of water. I would have to confront Joanie. Need I? To what avail? Were we finished together? I didn't think so. Gradually I became calm, gently pushed aside Joanie in my mind. Presley was urgent . . . Again I asked myself, why did I care about him? Who *was* he? It's an existential question not in vogue these days—you are who you say you are—but it had a certain potency here.

On my office pad idly I wrote,

> *The lion is out at midnight*
> *The fender of a red car*

An airport, people waiting
A baby's wide-eyed face peering through torren-
tial rain. Whose baby?
A bridal veil. White lace. Whose wedding?
A bookstore. Where? London? Why?
And bizarre: a cat barking
A man with red Afro hair, fair skin, who
likes yellow socks. Has an interest in the singer
Aboubakar Touré and—apparently—in the music
of Richard Wagner; and also in military games
and in weapons, but actually he is a reserved and
gentle person.
The hunter must stalk and kill the lion. A new
lion will stalk at midnight . . .

The last line was mine. I didn't know why I wrote it. I pushed away the pad, got up, and suggested to Lamar that we go down to the cafeteria. As we sat at our table with our lunch, he said,

—I found a device stuck to your jacket. A ladybug.

—You threw it away?

He shook his head slowly and flashed a tricky smile.

—No. I removed it and stuck it on your left sleeve, under the first button. You can remove it when you need to. That okay?

—Smart man.

—It can listen too.

—I know.

—And take pictures.

TWENTY

LATER THAT AFTERNOON in the midst of my consultations a call arrived from the Department.

—Dr Sina, have you heard from your patient Presley?

It was Joe Green on the line, all business today, the phone lending a pitch to the voice.

—No, Joe, I haven't heard from him—I'm worried.

The concern slipped out because it was real.

—And there's cause to worry, said Joe.—His condition could get dangerous, as we both are aware, and his life may be threatened. So if he contacts you, please, without delay—

—Joe, has it occurred to you folks that he has not contacted you because maybe he doesn't trust you?

—Why wouldn't he trust us, Dr Sina? We are his guardians . . . all we want is to find him so we can cure him . . .

Do you know something we don't, Dr Sina?

—Just a thought, Joe. The Department sometimes scares off people, as you know . . . Could you let me know if *you* find him? I am genuinely concerned.

There followed a significant pause. Right at that moment, I guessed, he was watching me on a screen . . . or someone else there was . . . or perhaps a team had gathered, observing intently, gauging my reactions and drawing conclusions.

—Dr Sina . . .

—Yes?

—Of course we'll inform you if we find him.

—Thank you.

—But I must tell you it is more urgent now than before that we find Presley Smith. If he contacts you, please get in touch immediately. You will be saving more lives than just this one.

—I don't understand. Whose lives, besides his?

—Let's leave it at that for now. Just remember what I've said. Goodbye, Doctor.

With that, he hung up.

An eerie thought: whose lives besides Presley's were at stake and why? Presley had now become larger than before, but when he first came to see me he had been only a man with a curable problem.

A patient who'd transgendered wanted to remember a happy suburban childhood as a girl—running in the wheat fields of Iowa, pigtails flying, dog chasing after her. She (as he now was) had even brought a poster with her illustrating this desire . . . corduroy overalls, check shirt . . . Why do people desire a storybook Midwestern idyll in their past? Or one in an English countryside? Why do so many wish to have been Elizabeth Bennet, Mr Darcy, or Anne of Avonlea in their previous lives? Unfortunately for them that's chronologically impossible, you cannot wish away a century and more. This patient was second generation, and there were complications. The feet were still large, so were the knees. The jaw line was too strong, and the voice not perfect, it rarely is. But the physical aspect of personality was not my department. Memories were, and some that need erasure were simply too strong—how do you submerge an inner-city hood's life inside a large, cozy family? That was for me to fix. My client today was not a hood, and hers was in principle an interesting case, but I struggled with a sense of irritation. I saw myself asking, why this vanity, why the lies? And yet I knew they were necessary; in this particular case there was a history of abuse. Psychological wounds need cosmetics too, and some lives need total abandonment. Excision. We discussed procedures, set up appointments.

Lamar came in to remind me that the next morning he would accompany our patient Dr Erikson to set him up in his new life. The doctor would leave the clinic a new immigrant and begin life again. Among his antecedents he counted a motor rally driver who'd raced in Africa. Of his previous origins— But I should not reveal more. Of course he had prepared himself before assuming this new identity, and he would be welcomed and assisted by a new citizens' organization. I would go and see him off, I told Lamar.

Sheila Walktall came in, looking triumphant, I thought. But she was happy to see me. She had made a case for escaping from her present life, which involved unbearable trauma. We discussed schedules and procedures for her transformation. She had already made preparations—deposited funds for the new persona, given that entity a part-time job at the broadcaster where she herself worked now, and had made plans to move to a warm place in a short time. She would remain a tennis player and golfer and become interested in bridge. She had given herself a glorious-sounding name and designed her looks: brown hair in place of black, a more angular face with high cheekbones, elegant ears closer to the skull; and an inch or two more in height.

—Well, Sheila, you have your wish. Good luck.

—Thank you, Doctor. You are the best. In spite of your reservations, you understand and show consideration.

I dared not ask her about her children.

At the Brick Club later I first subjected myself to a squash match. My opponent that day was Salman Khan, one of the club's virtual pros. Our games were matched: even though he was a strapping muscular fellow, my placing and control, despite my joints, compensated for his strength and agility. Perhaps I was being patronized. This time I lost 0–3, my excuse being that I found his sudden mocking appearances on court, out of the glass walls, no fun at all. It didn't help either that while serving the ball he hummed a tune. After a shower I went to the dining room, wobbly but refreshed. As the waiter took me to the table where Joanie awaited,

I wondered if I detected a smirk on his face, for I knew that on other days she brought the mysterious Friend here. On those days I stayed away by our mutual, unstated understanding. But today was mine.

—You played Salman, she said. She could always tell.

—He won by simply irritating me. That's his game strategy.

—A psychological strategy—*you* should know better than to fall for it.

—And he goes after every ball, so you have to be in the right mood to beat him. Today I wasn't.

—We'll see to your mood, she smiled.—You should ask to play with the other Khans. Aamir is more your type, I think.

—Shahrukh isn't bad either.

The three resident virtual pros, VPs, are all called Khan, because apparently in the past an Asian family of Khans had dominated the sport.

—I'll have the last word, I told her.—I think I'll have tandoori salmon today.

She broke out into a wonderfully musical peal of laughter that couldn't but attract envious attention to our table.

—I told you, he's catchy, Salman Khan!

—I guess he is. And the other Khans are not edible.

—I could have the amaretto cake for dessert . . . no.

She was wearing a lovely yellow shirt, open at her slender neck. I didn't recognize it, or the modest little ruby at the neck.

She put a finger to it.—You gave it to me, when we first met.

—I did?

—Yes.

The room was dimly lit, candles at the tables. From the adjoining lounge came the quick beat of a Latino number, to which couples could be seen dancing. Such a life—a challenging and satisfying job, in which you made your contribution to the good of all, for which you were appreciated and duly rewarded, and a retreat at the club to de-stress with people of your calibre—and a beautiful, sexy partner—why wouldn't one wish to prolong it? Surely the mad mysticism of Professor Kumar and his companions must come from deprivation and envy, so that all this privilege could be dismissed as meaningless ephemera, and a future life must be projected where one was really better off?

—What are you staring at?

—I was thinking how privileged all this—this life is. The food, the wine, the candlelight . . . all this beauty . . . you . . . and the three Khans to play a sport with and cuss. It's only when—

—What? When what, Frank? Tell me.

—When there's a rupture in this neat fabric and another world floods in . . .

—I'm not sure I understand . . .

What I was saying, in part, was obvious, that no sense of euphoria lasts forever, a happy moment lasts only that moment. But there is a sense of calmness and equilibrium possible—which I had attained even with the knowledge and ache of Joanie's infidelity—until Presley Smith stepped in. Or was it always coming, this rupture that threatened to destroy that calmness?

She leaned forward and looking straight at me said in a soft voice,—I don't want you to abandon me, Frank.

We didn't say anything more as I mulled over this. I knew she meant it, and an emotion constricted my throat. I glanced away to dry the gleam in my eyes, then turned to her and, struggling to remain composed, I asked the question that had been burning inside me all day.

—Wouldn't you rather I went away? Disappeared? Made space for someone of your generation . . . ?

—How can you say that, Frank?

—I saw you at the protest at Yonge and Eg today.

—You . . . were there? What were you doing there?

—I was there looking for someone . . . You were quite forceful, though I didn't hear what you—

—I just went along with a friend . . .

—And that friend wants someone like me dead and gone?

—It's not that, Frank. You know it's about jobs and security. People of my generation can't find jobs. All those GNs everywhere. And the politicians have just given themselves a raise. Now that's enough to get people to come out and protest!

Not only to themselves, the politicians also gave raises to civil servants, including me, looking out for their own, which is how I could afford to be here at the Brick having wild salmon and excellent wine after a game of squash.

—I want you always to be with me, Frank. I mean it, she said.

—I'm always with you.

—You've been distracted these last few weeks, Frank. You go to your study and into your own world—when you think

I've fallen asleep. I don't know what's in your mind . . . who
you are . . .

　—It's a patient. It'll work out, don't worry.

　—Just one patient?

I nodded.—Don't worry, Joanie.

The hostage crisis, eclipsed momentarily by the Karmic
Four, was back in the headlines. Politicians continued to
blame each other, past incidents were dredged up, the president and the prime minister made threats and the pope
made pleas to the kidnappers. Tearful friends and relatives
appeared one by one in the media to beg for mercy for their
loved ones: *think of your own loved ones, your own children;
we should be friends, not enemies , , We do not represent our
government . . . we agree that immigration should increase
and there should be more exchanges between us . . .* Aerial
photos were displayed of the Warriors' compound that
housed the hostages, apparently in underground quarters.
Naval ships had started converging towards the problem
area. A rescue mission was briefly discussed, before the idea
was dropped, at least in public. Negotiations went on. And
time was running out, said Holly Chu from Maskinia, in her
latest transmission to the media, sitting behind a table in the
open, her automatic comfortably beside her. She repeated
the demands: cash in WCUs, equivalent amount in gold, in
exchange for the peeping Tom prisoners. Or else. She did
not say what, but we were reminded of the savage fates some
hostages had met in the past. Would they do the same to the
women and few children in their hands?

We watched the news together, Joanie sitting partially on my lap, and when Bill Goode came on she turned around to face me. She slipped out of her pants, and helped me out of mine. She placed a touch of aphrodisiac on my tongue and turned to the tube.

—What d'you think of *that*, Bill?

Bill Goode gave his trademark doughy grin.

In bed she slept on my arm, and soon that gentle, even snoring, that sonorous throb of life inside that beautiful long body began, to which I spent a long time listening. It was music. And then I released myself, padded off to my study.

The day had promised such trauma, and it had ended so blissfully. Still, like a sleepwalker I was drawn to that other life, these other characters who were so different from me, from another world almost. And I called needless risk upon myself. What I wrote was open to scrutiny, in principle, though Tom had promised me privacy. Why didn't I simply go on being a good citizen, keep faith in the authorities entrusted to look out for us, and accept the privilege and prestige I'd been given for my hard work and diligence?

Don't abandon me, she said. Was this abandonment, I sitting there staring at the screen, she in the bed, my place beside her empty and cold? Even with its flaws and fragility, wasn't the warmth of that bed worth more than anything else, wasn't that what humankind has always striven to protect? What kept bringing me here like some zombie in front of this desk, into this solitude of imagination, into this . . . this . . . lonely portal to a world . . . somewhere else?

TOM: *Welcome, Frank.*

FRANK: *Thanks.*

TOM: *What can I do for you?*

FRANK: *Could you give me a lowdown on Maskinia. A summary, modern times. Please.*

TOM: *Will do, Frank.*

FRANK: *And Aboubakar Touré.*

TOM: *Certainly! I'll even compile an album of songs for you! I'm also a fan!*

FRANK: *Thank you.*

TOM: *Do you need anything more on the lion? Or the red car, Frank? And Holly Chu is quite the obsession everywhere.*

FRANK: *No. Just look away, Tom, as you promised.*

TOM: *All right, Frank. Go ahead. Happy indulging!*

But far from happy or satisfied, I had become tense and nervous, though I tried to hide this from the inquisitive Tom. Why had he so casually brought up Holly Chu in conjunction with the lion and the red car? Was it to send me a signal—surely he didn't make errors?—that I was more closely observed than I had imagined? My sessions with him; my written imaginings, my free and innermost thoughts; and the jottings I typed in my notepad at the clinic—they were all monitored. I had been naïve and reckless, saying, as most people do, How long do you keep looking over your shoulder? Stop fretting and keep going on, what do you have to hide? My thoughts.

Now that I had been alerted, for which silently I thanked Tom, I decided to resort to paper and pencil for anything I considered personal. A cumbersome method, and I could ill afford to be seen using it. I did not know what else to do. Would the Cyliton guess? Probably, but I would feed him tidbits here and there and hope to put him off for a while. It had become imperative too to create an account of the Presley case—what transpired from the moment he walked into my office with that persistent random thought in his mind. That single, enigmatic sentence. Presley's story needed to be told, I resolved, and in a form that could not in one instant be erased. A man, a mind, a story should not be made to vanish without a trace.

Holly Chu's site hadn't changed much in appearance. All her recent transmissions to the media were linked, in which she talked to the world, making accusations and demands. The young can be naïve and too quick to be led, but they are less fettered by the need to self-preserve. The Freedom Warriors' activities were summarized; the head of the organization was referred to as the Nkosi. No photo was given of him, but there were several of Holly's new companion—whom I have called Layela—a striking woman, tall and slim with a long, straight nose, curly braided hair, and a bewitching smile. The message section on the site was a tangle of monologues, dialogues, and babble, with diatribes, abuses, and counter-abuses—it's easy to love and hate at a distance—in the midst of which I found embedded this little fragment:

My man. 4113 Walnut Street is where the party is. Help!
Leon.

Had they already seen it, this throbbing link to Presley Smith, man on the run?

There came a shuffle behind me and I turned around and saw Joanie standing at the doorway in her underwear, watching me. She gave a shiver. I went to her and took her in my arms.

—It's all right, I murmured.—Don't worry.

—Is it that patient?

—Yes. I'll have to go see him tomorrow.

—Shouldn't he come to see you—if he must?

—He can't. I'll explain everything later, Joanie. Trust me.

And we went back to bed.

In the morning Presley's face was on the news, on every interface, personal and public, described as an escapee from a mental ward who could be dangerous. With his features, he could hardly be missed.

TWENTY-ONE

The Notebook

#49

The Journalist

Holly bowed and took the elder's delicate brown hand and put her lips to it. She noticed the thick gold ring on his finger, carved with the insignia of what she thought was a lion head. A sweetly seductive perfume wafted from him. The cap on his head looked hand-embroidered, brown and blue. Framed by his white beard and curly hair, his face had a lovely dark glow. His deep brown eyes were warm and kindly. He reminded her vaguely of her grandmother. She stepped back and moved to a side.

The chief, Nkosi, asked,—What's your name, my daughter?

—Holly, she replied. She was surprised that the old man spoke in English.

—Haali. Good, the old man said, his eyes twinkling. He had a throaty voice, somewhat higher than she expected. It was bright and burning hot in the compound, and one of the young men there turned on a fan for him, which was quite useless. No, the old man said, he did not want to go inside into the air conditioning. He turned again to Holly with affection and said,

—You are Haali, but your Warrior's name will be Umoja wa Kwanza. Understand?

—Yes, Nkosi, Holly replied.

—It means unity *first*. We are a very disunited people. This faction fights that one, and that one fights someone else, who betrays us . . . He grinned slyly.

—Yes, Nkosi.

—You have come here, Umoja, to open for your people a window into our world. Isn't that so? This is what they are, you tell them. What do you expect to see? And when you've seen, then what? When you've shown them, then what? Will our condition change to become like yours? Never mind, we will show you our world. Stay, and you will see starvation and disease, and radiation blight. You will see children with eight fingers or two heads and men who have cooked and eaten other men. Such is our world, which we cannot leave because your governments have put a fence around us. We live inside a cage.

—Yes, Nkosi.

—Don't just say *Yes Nkosi*! Do you believe me, Haali? Will you work for me?

—I believe you, Nkosi, and I will work for you.

#50

It's out, Presley, your link with Holly. Nothing is coincidence. It took the Cyliton to figure out your secret. I refused to see it. What are you, then, Pres, a terrorist from Maskinia? A Freedom Warrior? Does that explain your war games? *Many lives are involved*, Joe said, so will you regain your former self, pick up a gun, and go on a rampage? I don't think so, Pres, that's not possible. Your mind is now a jumble of two selves, a no-self overloaded with details, data, crying out in agony in that hole in which you've hidden yourself.

My fear is, Pres, there's even more to you that's staring me in the face. Some truths we'd better not know.

Slowly it's becoming clear to you, where you hide nursing your own internal terror, your incoherent, chaotic mind screaming with noises and blinding with images, what the meaning is of that statement. *It's midnight, the lion is out.* You see yourself driving the red car. But whose baby is in the rain?

TWENTY-TWO

IF HE SOUGHT SOMEWHERE to lose himself, he had chosen the right neighbourhood. What connection could he possibly have to Walnut Street, I wondered as I made my way there. Nothing had brought me this far east before, though like most people I was aware of the area's reputation. Crime is so rampant in this part of Lawrence Town that it registers only as a colourful instant of diversion from more important news. Reports from Walnut Street, as we know, invariably involve flashing lights and wailing sirens. A good place to hide, then. To reach it I had been careful about being followed—hurriedly crossing roads and changing directions, walking well inside shadows and in the middle of crowds, and once even getting off and back on the train—knowing full well that these antics were useless, not to say comical.

There are more efficient ways to track a person. Even the air we breathe has eyes, they tell us. There was that ladybug planted on my jacket, and though I was not wearing it now, there could well have been something else stuck to me or that I had ingested.

I emerged from the dank dungeon of a station from another century into a world that was alien and truly depressing, and hurried nervously further east down Walnut Street in the direction of increasing numbers. The brighter, commercial section of Lawrence Town was two blocks behind me on Prince Albert Park Avenue, but Walnut Street was dark and dismal, pressed down by a foggy night. Wet potholes lurked like traps to break your legs, street lamps were sporadically lit. The buildings were of yellow or brown brick and of two or three storeys. Many windows were boarded.

There was once some hope brought here, one is told, when immigrants were arriving by the planeloads, many choosing to settle in Lawrence Town. Developments sprang up. But Walnut Street failed to prosper, and those who did well left the neighbourhood. Now it is our Forgotten World. We fret about the Long Border and Region 6, we drop aid to those countries and are constantly in confrontation with them, our media never tire of describing and debating about their miseries. But this border world in Lawrence Town is our own, and it might as well not exist; it's too embarrassing, too ugly. Not exotic or exciting enough for Holly Chu, though surely unsafe enough.

A homeless man looked up from a steaming manhole and called out for change before closing the lid over himself; a couple of decrepit old women out on a walk with a little dog gave me a wide berth. A strip mall with a convenience store, a fast-food place, and a little Indian restaurant called Something-India—there was no other business on the street. A police car was one of two vehicles parked there. Lamar had advised me not to bring anything of value and so I had with me only a couple of paycards and an old phone that he had given me for this journey, used previously by a client who was no more—or rather was someone else. Not strictly legal to use these, but it's handy.

On the steps of 4113, two men sat in the shadows, smoking joints and chatting, ignoring me completely, so that I had to step gingerly between them to get to the door behind. I was the wrong sort here, and looked it. A murmur of contempt followed me in as I pushed through the door into a small vestibule, and saw a row of broken old mailboxes and buzzers beside an inner door. I pushed it in and took the staircase up. The lighting was the barest minimum. A woman came down scolding a child behind her, and brushed past me in her scratchy old coat. This was a house more than a century old; the stairs creaked, the bannisters swung out alarmingly at the slightest push, the walls were the colour of vomit; and indeed a fetid odour, heightened by some cheap deodorizer, permeated the entire dark cavern, along one side of which the stairs reached up to the residence corridors. As I climbed up, on the third floor a woman shouted, two children screamed and started running down, shaking the wooden structure of the house to its foundations.

Reaching the first floor before they did, I knocked on apartment 3 and a door was opened by a short, bent, aged-looking woman, with red hair cropped to the skull and a dark face shrunken as a raisin. She hobbled off inside and I stood at the entrance facing Presley Smith, who was sitting on an armchair which had been turned at an angle so he could watch the wall-mounted flat television. He looked up sideways at me and grinned.

—You made it, Doc.

—Yes—though I wondered if I would. What's this place?—you don't live here?

I closed the door, just as the floors trembled from the chase proceeding down the staircase. There was also in the room a long, low sofa with a white cloth cover, on which had been thrown assorted clothes, and two straight-backed chairs and a centre table. The floor had been polished decades ago, probably when the walls were also papered. A chandelier hung from the ceiling but the dim light in the room came from a floor lamp and the flickering television.

—My hideout, Doc. My hideout, he replied a little edgily.

His red Afro had collapsed somewhat from lack of care and lost its lustre. His clothes looked unwashed. Presley seemed to fit in here, but it was hard to suppress my revulsion. I was not sure that my concern for my patient had warranted this risky and unpleasant venture. He was eyeing me curiously, watching my discomfort. I couldn't even decide where to sit. Such places have insects, I'd been told, and not the nice sort. I couldn't help recalling Bill Goode making his insect gesture on his show.

—Were you followed? he asked.

—I tried not to be. There's no guarantee against the experts. A police car's hovering outside.

—I see. Mrs Clarke, Edwina—he nodded towards the kitchen, from where a sound came—agreed to take me in. She's my former girlfriend's mother.

Edwina hobbled in with a tray of tea and biscuits. She looked at me with a tight-lipped smile and a hard glitter in her eyes. I took the tray from her and placed it on a side table.

—Thank you, son, she said, which was indeed flattering.—Have a seat, she added,—have a seat.

I sat down on one of the two chairs, watched her pour the tea shakily into cups and lay out the biscuits. She was a black woman. I realized now what I implicitly had known, that there were areas of the city known for being pure ethnic, one of those that journalists like to visit on occasion to show their audiences glimpses of the *authentic*. If this was authentic, who wanted it?

I accepted a cup from her and Presley took his. We watched her leave the room.

—Mrs Clarke, aren't you going to sit with us? I called out.

—You go ahead and have your talk, she said and disappeared.

Presley and I sat in silence for a while, appraising each other. He did not look distressed; on the contrary he looked definitely upbeat.

—How are you faring? I asked him.—You sounded desperate in your message, but you seem to have managed. Have you?

—I'm managing, but mark you, with a lot of concentration and willpower. Edwina's concoctions are helpful. He nodded towards the kitchen.—She makes tea from extracts that she buys from a Chinese doctor in the neighbourhood.

He started to say something else, but stopped.

—So you can control those stray thoughts that bothered you before. That's very good, Pres. Maybe we doctors can learn from that!

And we could have met in the city, I thought. All that effort and risk to come see him, for nothing. He read my face and apologized.

—I'm sorry, Doc. You had to come all this way. When I posted that message I *was* desperate. There seemed no hope. But soon after, I began to improve. I found I can keep the lion away. The lion who stalks at midnight! It always starts with him—the lion. I keep him at bay. Stay away, lion!

He grinned, having gestured with his hand to shoo away the creature.

The scientist in me wanted desperately to record him. What he said in his current state could be of value to my discipline. But I was forgetting myself. He was my patient, who needed attention. I listened carefully to him, aware that I'd recall most of it later. And what I'd just heard was not reassuring at all. It sounded forced.

—DIS is desperate to see you, Pres. There's a call out on you. For all we know, there's a camera pointing at us.

We both threw a look towards the window, but it was

totally barred to the outside.

—Thank you for coming—and caring—Doc. I didn't trust you at first, when I came to see you, but now I see that I can. I think I'll be all right with the people here. They look after me—Edwina and others.

—It's not a trivial condition we are speaking of.

—Yes. But I'm managing. There's the Chinese potion, and I do yoga to strengthen my mind. All that seems to work. And I attend the church here. The community feeling, Dr Sina, has given a new meaning to my life. I did not have it before. I was alone. Now I really belong, Doc. I have friends and I have community.

This was the second time he was shunting me away, after first seeking me. But he'd found a meaning and a way to cope—so he believed. But the brain is a canny beast, I told myself. I didn't know what more to say and we both sat there in uncomfortable silence, listening to a burst of sirens go screaming past outside.

—You'll live in hiding.

He looked at me as though to say, What alternative do I have?

I was ready to leave.

—I've brought some pills for you, Pres. They will help suppress those flashes. First take the blue one, then the yellow one—if you need to. Let's hope you don't.

—Thanks, Doc. I hope so too.

He smiled. And in that face, behind that smile, suddenly I didn't see any hope at all. I could never forget that face, what destruction it revealed behind that mask.

—I should go, then, I said and got up.—I hope you'll be all right, Pres.

—I trust you, Doc. Believe me. I'm as all right as it's possible to be. And I'm happy and with friends. They are my family.

I wondered in what condition I would see him next. We shook hands. As I reached the door, Edwina opened it for me, and as I stepped out, she murmured,

—Can you make me young, Doctor? Like him and you. But no ghosts. I don't want to be visited by ghosts.

—There's no guarantee against ghosts, Edwina. And it's very expensive.

—Well then.

She let me out, and the locks clicked several times behind me. I went downstairs and out into the street.

As I hurried down the street, blaring metallic music approached from ahead followed by a car packed with punks. Before I could thank my stars that they hadn't stopped to harass me, another car came along and stopped.

—Whitey!

I'm not exactly white, and besides, these descriptions long lost their use in the society I come from. I kept walking.

—Whitey—you got any money on you?

—Not for you.

It's easy to sound bold, but my legs were quaking.

Two doors opened and two hulking fellows came loping towards me. The one in the lead, who had spoken, I now saw was as white as chalk with tattoos on his arms. There was metal in his teeth. His hands were metal contraptions, in one of which he held a small zapper, and I was thinking, This is it. I looked behind me, desperate for someone to come to my rescue. The young man laughed. He waved his zapper, though he didn't need it, with one swing of that psychedelic arm he could have felled me. What would he do then, drink my blood? Cut me open and steal my organs? (Fine use they'd be.)

—What have you got in your pockets?

I fetched out one of my paycards and my phone. He pocketed the paycard and snatched at my phone, which with a quick glance he threw contemptuously on the ground and stepped on it. Not his fashion.

Just then a police car, which seemed to have been lurking in the shadows, slowly came cruising along and the two men jumped into their car and sped away. The police car stopped beside me.

—What are you doing here, sir?

—Visiting a friend who's sick. She used to work for me. Mrs Clarke . . .

—Any ID?

—I'm afraid not. I was told not to bring anything that had value.

I told them who I was, gave them my phone numbers.

—You have to be careful. Strangers have a way of disappearing in these streets. You could end up in a hamburger.

They chuckled, and I didn't know if they were serious, but they remained in sight until I entered the station.

As Joe Green had said, sometimes we need the police.

TWENTY-THREE

The Notebook

#51

The Journalist

Holly lay on her mattress in her corner. She had strung up a rag of a bedsheet as a makeshift curtain to demarcate her space, an indulgence allowed her by her new friends. She could sleep only lightly at night. The space was utterly dark; immersed in it, at first she felt nervous and frightened. This was the price of her privacy. But gradually she was getting accustomed to her space, to the intermittent scratches and sighs that relieved the brief loneliness of the night. She would think of the comfortable world she had left behind, rejected and spurned. Had she made the right decision? Yes!

At some point you have to stop talking and do something, take that first step. And she had done that. If more people did likewise, the world might change. Hadn't that fellow Gandhi inspired millions?

A squeal came from behind the curtain, a slight one, and it brought her suddenly fully awake. She sat up and listened. There were growls. Men. Shuffling. Then three men stepped in, lifting the curtain; the space now lighter, she saw shadows and recognized the men, she had seen them around. One of them came over and pointed a rifle at her and she was terrified. Another swiftly approached her, bent down, and grunting tore off her pyjamas—which were recently stitched, a gift from Layela. When he'd had his way, not one word escaping her lips, her eyes locked into his, her heart bursting with pain, the two others followed. They left, summarily zipping up themselves. As she whimpered in pain and filth, Layela took her into her arms and comforted her; took her outside and hosed her, and she cried out.

—Shall I complain to Nkosi? she asked her friend.

—You should, replied Layela.

—You should, said Miriam.—Perhaps then he'll listen.

In the morning they went marching with determination to the Nkosi's compound. The soldiers teased them on the way, and at the gate they were met with hostility: Nkosi was busy, Nkosi was tired, there was a big meeting today. But the women persisted, Miriam speaking loudly to be let in, until suddenly the gate opened for them.

Nkosi was seated in his chair as usual, having at that moment finished with a tall glass of juice. The three women sat down on the ground before him, and after a preamble Holly told her story.

—I've treated these men as brothers in arms, as fellow warriors, and they have shown no respect for me and violated me. They don't respect women—

—Haali, Haali—began the old man,—they should not have touched you. I am sorry. They will be punished.

He paused, then went on.—We are fighting a war, Haali. We need young, healthy warriors. Men. They need to eat . . . You go, I will punish them.

Holly didn't know if and how the men were punished. She never saw them again. But Layela and Miriam told her this was the way of their world. The women had to yield, the young men had to eat, most of them would soon go to die.

#52

The Gentle Warrior

And you, Presley, you almost fooled me—but not quite. We both know, no Chinese medicine, no Christian piety, no Indian exercises will save you. I wish I could have helped you, my friend. My young friend. The moment I laid eyes on your incongruity, some nerve in the visual cortex rang a bell. Some memory circuit responded, albeit weakly, I admit. We are connected, you and I . . . and for sure Holly.

TWENTY-FOUR

MASKINIA.

A vaguely defined area of Region 6 troubled by poverty, disease, civil wars, and corruption. Formerly it was occupied by sovereign nations that had achieved independence from European dominance in the twentieth century. The name of Maskinia is believed by some scholars to be derived from *masikini* or *miskin* (South Asian and African languages, through Arabic) meaning a beggar, or someone deserving charity. Other, less demeaning and exotic etymologies have been suggested. The languages spoken are numerous: they include variants of English and French, Swahili, Arabic, Hausa, Lingala, Bambara, and others of indigenous origin. An evolved Hindi is spoken by a small minority.

To the southeast of the region lies EAF, the East African Federation; the other boundaries are more fluid, and the region, described loosely, overlaps with the former Congo, which has been torn by strife for well over a century. Maskinia is rich in minerals, predominantly uranium and gold, and agricultural land that for reasons explained below cannot be fully exploited. Despite its natural wealth, Maskinia by all measures of development remains one of the poorest areas in the world, the majority of the population earning less than five dollars a day and lacking basic amenities such as electricity, running water, and sewage disposal. It has progressively lost any semblance of government, having long fragmented into warring factions and chiefdoms. This condition has been exacerbated by the imposition of the Long Border to stop the tides of desperate migrants sweeping upon European and American shores.

The current misery of Maskinia has its genesis in the year 2032. Before then the region was at the height of its so-called Southern Resurgence, a period of economic prosperity and relative peace. In 2032, however, for reasons yet to be clarified, two of the region's nations, Garibu and Tajiri, declared war on each other. In the midst of hostilities, two 1000-megawatt nuclear reactors of Canadian design, operating in tandem, mysteriously exploded. This catastrophe, known as the Great Explosion, brought an end to the war, but the region never recovered. The incident caused considerable damage, which went uncontrolled; faulty Canadian design was blamed, and the angered populace turned on the experts that were sent to assist. Secondary explosions were not prevented. Endangered populations were not removed in time. Since then, unexpected weather patterns with large-scale flooding have extended the contamination areas. The food and water consumed, unless donated by aid agencies or grown in artificial soil, is largely unsafe.

The biological effects of the nuclear catastrophe include low birth rates, male impotency, deformities at birth, high rates of cancer, and the emergence of new species, including a large version of the domestic cat. Life expectancy has dropped from a high of sixty-seven to fifty-five.

Shortage of cultivable land has led to large-scale internal migrations, resulting in ethnic and religious strife and the emergence of three regional militias, the Freedom Warriors, the Army of the Hungry Christ, and the animist New Mau Mau. Tighter clampdown and casualties at the Long Border are a cause of bitter resentment, used to advantage by the militias to rally for recruitment into their ranks.

The Freedom Warriors in one form or another has controlled the central portion of Maskinia for over thirty years, with its headquarters in a suburb of Sinhapora. It is considered by most world governments to be a terrorist organization, though it fulfills its social mandate by providing limited health services and education. Its strength has varied over the years. Its activities have included abductions; attacks on development and aid networks; attacks on industrial activities such as mining; smuggling people to the north; and drug trafficking. From time to time it leaks out personnel through the Long Border to carry out acts of terror. In two instances precision attacks on the headquarters almost destroyed the organization, but it re-emerged after a period underground. Diplomacy and gifts (bribery) have not been effective because the FW leaders rarely keep their word for long. A hands-off approach combined with Border vigilance, sanctions, and selective punishment (military action) is the current policy in place and known as the Macmanus Containment Doctrine.

The FW has always been led by a charismatic dictator, called Nkosi, the Leader, under whom is an unelected council, called a Baraza, of seven people. The Nkosi is elected by the Baraza from its members. The present Nkosi is Eddy Noor, a much-loved elder of benign visage and saintly aura who is yet responsible for initiating many recent acts of terror and sabotage. A crafty politician, his ability as negotiator and intermediary has found use by the Northern Alliance and enabled him to survive and forestall punitive attacks.

The Warriors grew out of an Islamic fundamentalist organization militantly opposed to the Western way of life. In recent times, however, while adhering to a few previous prohibitions such as those against drinking, and promoting austere lifestyles, it has stayed away from overt Islam, allowing instead for the syncretistic cultures and modes of worship that have emerged from the large-scale upheavals, migrations, and admixtures of populations following the Great Explosion.

The Warriors run rudimentary primary schools in Maskinia and one high school near their headquarters in Sinhapora. The last punitive bombing of the headquarters resulted in the death of over a hundred boys and girls, a major public-relations setback for the North Atlantic Alliance. High school graduates have been known to attend universities in neighbouring countries, and due to the extreme conditions there has been a steady migration out of Maskinia.

The FW runs a basic hospital two miles away from its headquarters, with an estimated sixty beds. There are also at least four mobile medical units that tour the region.

The Warriors receive support from a small number of left-wing intellectuals in neighbouring countries. Volunteer doctors and teachers make their way in small numbers into Maskinia. There is also support from some radical groups of the Alliance countries who provide propaganda and channel funds in secret. Humanitarian agencies are also active in the region, most notably the World Development Network.

Maskinia's neighbours are believed to pay discreet protection fees to the Warriors. Abductions are a source of income, though they are rarely publicized.

The FW remains adequately armed with an arsenal of second-grade weapons purchased on the market. There is in place a simple, partially effective missile shield, purchased from the EAF. There also exists under the hills outside Sinhapora a system of deep, naturally formed tunnels that were extended and used for protection in the aftermath of the Great Explosion. The full extent of this maze is unknown. Several attacks by special forces to destroy the organization at its root have been foiled by the successful use of this tunnel system.

FRANK: *Thanks, Tom. That's quite comprehensive.*

TOM: *There's more.*

FRANK: *How much more?*

TOM: *Everything.*

FRANK: *Not everything now, but could I know more about the Nkosi—Eddy—bio, photos? Family? And the Baraza?*

TOM: *That information is protected, Frank. I will need a clearance.*

FRANK: *Okay.*

. . .

TOM: *Frank, you've disappointed me.*

FRANK: *Oh? How so?*

TOM: *Your creative musings. You are hand writing them now.*

FRANK: *Yes.*

TOM: *Rather a primitive method.*

FRANK: *But safe from prying eyes.*

TWENTY-FIVE

WE SUPPOSE OUR DNA to predispose us in certain ways—gift us with an artistic or scientific temperament, for example, or an exceptional ability in a sport. Yet the connection is not clear or precise. Nurture, training, plays a large role. A child of a medical doctor can go on to become a popular musician; the child of a trader becomes a scientist; and the child of a warrior a pacifist. The point of my lecture was, which of these proclivities or special traits in us can be suppressed or manipulated in the brain? Can the artistic temperament be switched off, for example, and a mathematical proclivity be turned on in its place? And further, can a certain genius survive a change of past history—as in the case of rejuvenation? If the deaf Beethoven, now cured of this and other ailments, wants to carry on in a new life, with a new memory of a happier childhood and love life as a youth, the symphonies he composes, were he able to do so, will be different, but will they be great? Is genius mutable?

The Henri-Persi College of Advanced Arts and Science had invited me to give its annual Raymond Lecture. The subject is of great interest at that distinguished college, and also to all with special gifts. It's understandable for an artist, a mathematician, or a chess grandmaster to want to carry their gifts with them into the next generation; for a Beethoven to carry his bag of tricks with him, so to speak. Some of them would rather die of age than risk losing their particular gift.

The hall was near full and the audience looked absorbed, which is always gratifying. Joanie was present too, seated in the second row. Even if I say so myself, I have a way with my audiences. Joanie says it's that special lilt and crackle in my voice that mesmerizes, by which I assume she means it possesses an aged, old-wine quality. I give more credit to my subject. We all age. As I began to wind up, I noticed Radha slip into the hall and find a seat in a middle row. Why come at all, if this late, was the thought that entered my head as I proceeded.

There are many questions, I told them, some of which have answers, others not yet. I can install in you a memory of a young Einstein—not the real one: he lived too long ago— but that will not turn you into an adult Einstein. Why? The memory of a lived life is different—it's real, it's *experienced*; detailed and nuanced and in important ways tangible. The nature of genius is still a mystery—which is a good thing, some might say; we cannot have more than one Einstein living among us at the same time. (Laughter.) There's the gender issue. Can a change of gender, with a new autobiography, preserve a predisposition? Can Marie, already a prominent chemist in Paris, become François and go on to discover radium? Then (I looked up) there's always someone who asks, Can you give me the memory of Child Jesus? Yes, but he would be in modern North America riding a bus instead of a donkey, and even then we can't guarantee that God will make you His son. Which is just as well. (Laughter.)

How far was this audience, how far their world from the one I had visited the other day, Walnut Street, cloaked in the dark aura of deprivation and danger. Concern for the indigent among us was brought up, not surprisingly by a young person. A woman in this case.—Since rejuvenation is available to the rich, what about the poor? What is their place in this Brave New World of yours? Is your science a method to cull the poor from our midst?

The answer is obvious and the same I give every time, that progress moves forward, not backward. We cannot unknow scientific knowledge, or undo technological advance—it is not in human nature, we are a competitive, speculative species. We should, however, be cautious in how we apply these advances—as we have been in the past with nuclear energy and animal cloning, when the dangers were always clear, but we could not do without their uses in the production of energy, food, and medicine. In the instance of rejuvenation, the answer to the questions raised is that it be available to all. We should not close our eyes to progress, but our attitudes should change. We should address poverty.

A professorial man, soft-featured and round-faced, wearing a blue blazer and topped with a white halo of hair on his otherwise bald head, half raised a hand next and asked, in a gently quavering voice,—Genius and ability are one thing, Doctor, but what about *a subject's beliefs*? Is there a proclivity towards fanaticism, for instance, an innate attraction for it, and can it be passed on, or indeed suppressed—have you identified such cases?

His air of confidence, the aura of authority, had become apparent to the audience, which had suddenly turned quiet. Beside him, I noticed, sat Joe Green.

To the question raised, I had this answer:—I've not identified fanaticism in itself as a trait to follow. I would say it's too vague a concept—you are a fanatic about *something*. However, the cases that come to us are what you might call cosmetic or vanity cases. All that our clients require are different—better or more romantic—pasts that they wish to remember as their own. A very mundane and understandable desire.

—You don't—excuse me for going on, Doctor—you don't get men or women with very strong beliefs—in Marx, or Allah, or Hanuman for example? In Jesus? Or with particular hatreds—those who hate with a passion—and who wish to carry on with . . . the passion? How do you deal with them?

There was much unsaid in that question, and I proceeded cautiously.

—I've not had clients who declared such beliefs—religious or political or any other—and wished to take them along into another life. If they harboured such passionate beliefs they would run the risk of losing them through their identity change. Of course, it's possible these specific passions would return into their new lives as intrusions or arbitrary thoughts in what we call the Nostalgia syndrome. The truly religious cases, in any event, would not come to us, already believing in an afterlife.

He nodded and mouthed, silently, *Of course.* But who was he? He seemed an important man. And now he began to look vaguely familiar. I must have run into him somewhere. It was my turn to question him:

—And you are, sir? You appear knowledgeable on the subject. Would you mind introducing yourself to the audience?

Somewhat startled, he looked around, then said,—I'm sorry, I should have done that earlier. My name is Axe— A-X-E. Dr Arthur Axe. From the Department of Labour.

He sat back, the exchange over, and the auditorium regained its background hum. Someone else had a question:

—Can you speak about Nostalgia?

This was easy, I proceeded to explain.

—The leaked memory syndrome, LMS, or the Nostalgia syndrome is the case in which stray thoughts that we believe are from a former life move into the head—leak in. Usually they are harmless and sometimes impossible to tell apart from other thoughts. Sometimes, though, they can multiply into a deluge, and immediate recourse is necessary.

Dr Axe was staring at me. He was smiling, his eyes twinkling, his look friendly, avuncular, and I took a moment to return a smile. At this same instance realization dawned upon my entire being, and a nervous frisson shot through me. He must have seen it on my face, my smile unfolding, my shoulders stiffening, and I could see the beam in his eye switch off. And I was as certain as Newton was when the apple fell on his head (let's suppose it did) that I was looking at the mysterious Author X, not from Labour but from Internal Security. The master ironist of the Publications Bureau. The one who wrote Presley's script, gave him his life. A great man, in a manner of speaking, to whom Joe Green, now sitting beside him, was merely an adjutant. Joe too took time to throw me a look of significance. They stood up and left in one abrupt coordinated motion, followed by a third person behind them.

He could have watched me on video, with a drink in his hand, in all his terrifying anonymity; in the leisure of his private club or at home. Why would this powerful man, whose mystery works to enhance his reputation and influence, this anonymous author make himself known to me? Was it simple miscalculation in an instance of an all-too-human weakness, arrogance? An author who wanted to be known this once?

I watched them depart through the side door, Joe Green turning to look back at me one last time. He seemed curious.

They must know that I'd tried to shake off their surveillance more than once (how successfully, I don't know), and therefore I could not be trusted. Did they know I'd met Presley? Had they found him?

I seemed to have been swallowed into a time hole, and emerged once more to face the audience.

It was now that my other set of monitors, the raucous ones, went on the offensive and finished ruining the event.

Just as the convenor rose to thank me, a young man jumped up and insisted on having his say. There was something of the eternal student in him, a swarthy and underfed man of small stature who'd not bothered to remove his coat. He sounded shrill.

—My name is Musa. My point is that while you, the elderly elite, find ways to prolong your existence with new organs and new lives and monopolize the world's resources, what about us young people? When do we get a chance? Youth unemployment is approaching thirty percent! I don't mind telling you that I cannot find a job—and the woman I love—a young woman, not a reconstituted senior citizen—lives with an elderly man—sells her services just to be able to survive! What gives people like you the right to more life than others? Why can't you just say, *I've had enough! Let others live!*

At this cue more of them sprang up in different parts of the hall, shouting *You've had enough! Get out! Blasphemy!* And Radha was one of them, but she was shouting about karma and flashed a somewhat guilty smile when our eyes met.

The young and the religious; if Dr Arthur Axe had stayed on to observe this scene, he would have been tempted to speak out,—You see? I mean *them*. Can the tendency for this behaviour be passed on? Would you let it happen? Would you want such people around forever?

A distressing conclusion, then. I'd never before been attacked so personally and in public for my beliefs and my practice. I keep a low profile, and speak publicly only when invited by special groups. Such meetings tend to be serious affairs. People come up and shake hands with me, others ask for references to my work. Admittedly, they are usually from the *elderly elite*—I'd not heard this description before, but to be perfectly candid, it seemed apt enough. But *reconstituted senior citizen*?

This night I had been ambushed by the G0s and the Karmics. The public lecture had been truly turned public.

As I stepped down from the stage, shocked and embarrassed, Joanie approached me with a reassuring smile and took my arm, just as I caught the angry young man Musa's hostile eye in the distance.

I gave her hand a squeeze.—Thanks for coming, darling.

—You did well. You had all the answers. Let's get out of here and celebrate.

—Let's.

While we were sharing this precious moment, Radha came gliding over, the face beaming as always.

—That was very interesting, Dr Sina. She turned to a curious and surprised Joanie, and continued,—Dr Sina's been visiting our protest site on Yonge Street, and I've been trying to convince him about why interfering with the karmic cycle is not such a good thing. It gives him bad karma.

—By *our*, you mean that group in which that man burnt himself to death?

—Yes.

—Ugh. Well, I hope you haven't succeeded in convincing Frank of your beliefs.

—I'm afraid not.

—Thank heavens.

The one trim and shapely, the lines clean as though drawn by an artist, with not an ounce of extra flesh, not an expression or move wasted, no fuzziness except on the rare occasions when she yielded to me. And the other, with a fleshiness that became popular briefly some years ago; all fuzzy, even her beliefs. Despite her karmic protests, she had looked decidedly shaken at Professor Kumar's self-immolation. She walked away, unperturbed.

As I turned towards Joanie, I caught Musa's somewhat furtive eye upon her. He looked away.

—Have you met that young man—Musa—before? He seems straight out of some anarchists' colony. He was staring at you very strangely.

—The one who skewered you—yes, I think so, somewhere.

Too quick, and a necessary half-lie, perhaps there lay *her* fuzziness. They had exchanged glances and her face had reddened. Musa, I was convinced, was the mysterious Friend she saw on the side. There was no point in asking what she saw in that scruffy man. *I love a young woman* . . . Which made me . . . what? The reconstituted senior citizen to whom she had sold herself. That was painful, that barb. Joanie, partly turned away, was looking blandly around the room with a baby's blameless face, and I was talking to an admirer while thinking, She can't see me that way . . . selling herself to . . .

Radha waved from a distance, sailing across the hall in her colourful sari.

It was not merely distressing that day, it was devastating.

Later that evening it was I who was cold, the aphrodisiac useless. I refused to rise.

TWENTY-SIX

The Notebook

#53

The Journalist

Haali, or Holly, had known when she kept returning repeatedly to Maskinia for XBN assignments, which were never imposed on her, that her fate was tied to that country; but she couldn't have imagined that one day she would identify with it so much. Before, she had come to the country as someone from a privileged planet, followed on the streets by packs of children like the Pied Piper, handing out cheap goodies from the North, stopping to take photographs and interview people; be admired and feel wonderful about herself; she was a *madam* from *there*. She ate special foods and

107

drank special water and constantly fortified herself against their touching. Now she was one of them and trusted. She ate and slept with them (though she had to be careful). She moved about freely exploring the neighbourhood, visited houses and played with the children, teaching them the rudiments of English; she trained with the women and ate with them, sitting in a circle on the floor, and made love with Layela. She was wary of the men, who needed *to eat*, but she was never touched by them again. She knew she would not return to America. As she listened to the Nkosi speak to his followers, his message always the same but explained in different ways, she came to believe in it, felt one with the others in this belief. It seemed so obvious. A small percentage of the people on earth wallowed in wealth while the rest suffered deprivation. She could see it all around her, the poverty and forbearance, and yet the kindness and a sense of humour and play. These people deserved better. There must be change, and she would play her small part to make that possible. And so when the Nkosi's men told her of their plan to waylay the tourist bus, using her as a decoy who would be trusted by the tourists, her former compatriots, she believed in its necessity for the greater good. The ransom would go a long way. She was moved to tears when she was handed her weapon in the presence of the Nkosi, a gesture of his complete trust in her.

She knew there would follow the inevitable negative responses from back home when she announced that she was a Warrior now and was staying on in Maskinia; still, the chorus of abuse that arrived was shocking to her. Sympathy and friendship had transformed in the blink of an eye into pure hatred, without a consideration for what her message was to the world, that the people behind the Border, in so-called Barbaria, were only human, we must not fence them off like wild animals. Among those few whom she counted especially close to her, her father begged her to return and spread her message from the safety of home. No one would blame her, he told her, her behaviour could be explained by the shock of her trauma and her sincerity; there were many people who believed as she did. Her mother kept silent. Her friends' messages all amounted to the same substance: Come on, Holly, you don't mean that! Come to your senses! Come home and all will be well. And then all converging to the annoyed brush-off: Please don't write or call. I think it's better we don't stay in touch anymore. Holly who? She had been naïve, but was learning. She was on the other side. There was no in-between.

At first the tourists had been delighted to meet her, one of their own. A few had heard the recent news that Holly Chu, XBN star reporter, had been captured and eaten in a particularly noxious neighbourhood in Maskinia. So you're alive, after all! Wonderful! They made jokes: Can I take a bite? A nibble in the ear? Then she led them to the leader, Nkosi, who she said wanted to welcome them in person and give them gifts. She told them a new policy of rapprochement was in the making between their nations. They arrived at the headquarters in their tour bus, and Holly herself led them through the gates and somehow connived that their three guards were delayed at the back of the group, where they were overpowered and disarmed. The tourists entered the compound and were fed and then informed that they were prisoners of the Warriors. There was screaming and shouting, the men attempted to fight and resist (some of them were trained in combat), but finally they all quietened. They were photographed and filmed and led inside through tunnels to their quarters, which had been made reasonably comfortable for them.

Soon after the tourists' capture, Holly went to see them and explain to them their situation, and her own. They cried, they screamed, they tried to tear her hair out when they realized how she had tricked them. They beseeched. Come to your senses, Holly, help us, these people are savages and cannibals, they will kill us. They tried to convert her. You are one of us, we are an advanced people, at least accept your identity, be with us. We should maintain a solidarity, a dignity. We represent our civilization. Your friends are barbarians, through no fault of theirs; it's decades of poverty. And it's in their genes. We come from a civilized heritage. They are cursed, they have no history, no civilization, no science of their own, no art.

We are your fans! We have seen you in the news, you've stood in our homes and spoken to us. My daughter did a project on you, you inspired her! McGill!—I was there, we overlapped! Where did you house? On the hill? Me too, and then the student ghetto? What street?

Why have you betrayed us and yourself?

Holly told them, I feel one of them and I want to work with them. My grandmother was from these parts. I used to hear stories about her and about a great railway. I'm not sure exactly where it was . . . or where she came from. If you think of them as savages and cannibals, with no civilization or human grace, why did you come to see them? To gawk at them and throw them crumbs?—this canned stuff and these phones and cheap gadgets?—and feel good about yourselves?

Nothing will happen to you, I guarantee that. With my own life. You will not starve and you will not be personally harmed. These people are not all rapists. But they want to use you as pawns.

She knew that some of these women would not be left alone. She paused. She felt queasy.

TWENTY-SEVEN

EDWINA'S DARK, CREASED FACE filled the screen, her close-cropped hair red like blood.

—Doctor, you've got to come. He's raving beyond control.

A quaver in the voice.

—I'm coming right away.

The conversation was undoubtedly monitored, but what did it matter now. It was the moment I'd expected and feared all along.

—Come to the church, Doctor. The one across the street from the apartment, the Holy Trinity. Oh, poor man, what a fate it is . . .

This last sentence muttered, as she looked away and hung up. It was midnight, who goes to church at this hour? But then, what did I know of church-going? Joanie lay asleep, undisturbed by the phone, or perhaps electing not to query. The evening had left us both silently aching.

I arrived on Walnut Street by taxi. A light drizzle fell. Through the cold wet screen of rainfall the street looked dark and empty but for the dismal all-nighter at the strip mall, outside which this time sat a burly guard enviably dressed to the head and holding a weapon against the ground. A few blocks away somewhere sirens went screaming in varying pitches. The church was a tall and ancient red brick structure with a square tower barely visible in the mist; a low wrought-iron fence enclosed it inside a scrappy yard, and a gate opened to a paved walkway. The entrance was in shadow. I pushed the heavy door open into a compact and dimly lit vestibule with a noticeboard on a wall. There was another door here, arched and imposingly antique, leading to the prayer hall; from inside came shouts and muffled voices. I pushed and entered the chamber, a cavernous space filled with rows of wooden seats on either side of the aisle, overhung with glaring plastic chandeliers that looked indecently small and recent.

Up front, below the stage—on which stood a lectern and a chair under a large green banner with a gold cross in the middle—were gathered some fifteen people. Edwina saw me and approached me at the back, rolling her heels as she hurried in small steps, and taking my hand she led me on the red runner directly to the front to see Presley Smith. The crowd parted to let us through.

Presley Smith was lying on the carpeted steps leading up to the stage, his face contorted in a grimace and covered with beads of sweat, his mouth open, spit trickling down his chin. His red Afro was squashed into a mop. A clown in distress. A tiny shivering ran in waves down his body, breaking sporadically into a twitch. His shirt was untucked and his shoes had been removed.

The pastor, a small man in a black suit, stood at the top of the steps and spoke directly to me.

—He's been gibberin nonsense, all gibberish and speakin in tongues. Perhaps you can understand him, Doctor.

—The session was on, full swing, everybody all going into a trance like, a man explained.

—Despite my warnings, 'spite my warnings, muttered Edwina, and I wondered what warnings she had made and to whom.

From what I could gather, the congregation had collected for the evening service, during which members would bring themselves occasionally into trances, responding to the reverend's promptings. Presley, however, failed to emerge from his state. He kept moaning for a period, startling the others, and then suddenly he staggered up to the front, and turning to face them he pleaded,—You must help me! Don't you see, you've got to help me! As a few people went forward to assist, he collapsed on the floor. He then started speaking incomprehensibly, what the pastor described as gibberish. They didn't know what to do.

Edwina was bending down to wipe Presley's face, still speaking, as everyone else stood well away from him.

—No tellin what's going to come out in his condition . . . *can't control myself,* he was saying, *my self wants to come out.*

That's exactly what he said, *my self wants to come out, out, out*... And he was speakin in that strange, devilish tongue—

She crossed herself.

There was a chorus of reports:

—*My father*, he said, *my father*—in English.

—And *lion*, I heard him say, *lion*.

—There, he's speakin again...

The men and women all shut up, as from Presley's mouth came the bewildering sounds of a foreign language, as if there were someone else inside him speaking in breathless moaning sentences. And I was thinking professionally, by habit, that I'd not had a case like this before; you can give someone a new memory but you can't give him a language... he must have been bilingual. The words tumbled slowly, vaguely out of that troubled face. And they began to have this effect on me, they drew me in, and I strained to listen, strained to listen, expecting that if I tried hard enough I'd understand them. I was not myself, I had no control over myself. This strange patois, I knew it somehow, but I could not understand it, having lost the key to its mystery. I knew there stood only the thinnest wall between us—between Presley and me, this language and myself—the locked door and the absent key.

I should not have been there. And yet I *had* to be there.

—Can you understand him, Doctor?

—No... of course not.

—Jesus Christ have mercy on him, said the pastor.

—Amen, came a reply, and then a babel erupted.

—He's possessed.

Edwina was still ministering to him, having put a foot cushion under his head.

—Speak English, my dear, speak the Lord's tongue so He understands . . .

—What's he saying, Swahili or something? Arabic?

—Aramaic. That's the tongue. That sure is.

—Lord knows . . .

—And you're right.

This was not the time to make sense, to pause and reason. I felt helpless. I could do nothing but comfort him, and be a witness to his struggle against himself. I had brought tranquilizers to help him, but he was beyond my reach. Someone gave me a push. People were all around me, all clamouring to listen to Presley muttering in his trance; and to touch him now, because somehow he was not the devil anymore but sacred and inspired. With more pushing and shoving, I found myself ejected to the back of the crowd like an intruder. I gestured to Edwina and pointed to the pills in my hand, and she came through the crowd to take them from me.

There came the wail of an ambulance outside, decreasing in pitch as it stopped. Flashing blue lights. Attendants in white came running in and pushed through the crowd. They laid Presley on a stretcher and rolled him away.

—Did you call an ambulance? Edwina asked me.

—No, I didn't. But someone must have . . .

—Now who did, I wonder?

The church had emptied in a hurry meanwhile and turned deathly quiet. A few lights went out. The pastor was below the stage, facing away from me, grey head bowed in prayer to the gold cross; he turned around and walked up to the door, ready to lock up.

—Come with me, commanded Edwina to me.

—Where?

—With me. I have to show you something.

—I have prayed for Mr Smith, said the pastor at the door, giving me a nod of sympathy.

—Thank you, Pastor. I am Dr Sina. Presley Smith was my patient.

—I'm Imamu Issa Jones.

We shook hands. His, cool and damp and striving to be firm. He kept holding on for a moment longer.

—Was it you who called the ambulance, Pastor? I asked him.

—No, it wasn't me. I thought you brought it jangling along with you, Doctor.

His tone said I should have, shouldn't I? I shook my head, I didn't.

—Good thing someone did, Edwina said in front of me, evidently feeling cold in her flimsy coat, and we left, saying goodbyes again.

Who were those uninvited efficient, white-clad attendants, and where had they taken Presley? There could be little doubt. The surprise was that the ambulance hadn't arrived before me. But Presley was beyond help, they could do nothing for him.

We crossed the road and climbed slowly up the creaking stairs to Edwina's second-floor apartment. As I sat down on the chair where I had last sat, she went to the kitchen and brought back a bottle of bourbon and two glasses.

We shared the bourbon and commiserated. I asked her about Presley. She said he had no one except his former girl-friend, Edwina's daughter, Jude. He did not say where he was from. Had he committed a crime, Edwina asked him, when he came to her seeking refuge. No, he replied. Then why was he hiding? Because I have a secret, he said. He looked help-less and she had no choice but to take him in, having deter-mined in her mind that he was harmless.

I recalled our last meeting. We both knew then that we'd not see each other again.

—I've got something for you, she said, and with a small heave got up and went to the mantelpiece. She returned with a small flat object, which she put in my hands.—It's his, she added. It was a very slim old-fashioned notebook with a metallic black cover. I flipped the pages and saw that he'd filled a few of them. There are not many who possess the skill to write by hand; we both did, apparently. But by this time I was beyond surprise. Presley's hand on the page was uneven and unsteady, and he had used capital letters only. On one page were some names, addresses, and phone num-bers; my entry had a strong underline. On another page he'd written a few perfunctory sentences: *My name is Amirul. I had a cousin who was my teacher called Elim. I loved him very much. I lived in a compound . . .*

Edwina said,—The anguished man. Possessed by the devil. And now he's in a mad hospital. You should have sent him there straight away, Doc . . . if he was your patient.

I looked at her, wondered why her attitude had hardened. Perhaps the foreign tongue had frightened her, made him a foreigner in her eyes. The whole episode had been an imposition on her meagre existence, a life I could barely even begin to imagine.

She told me I could sleep on the sofa the rest of the night, and at first I demurred. But Joanie would be asleep anyway, I figured, and so I took the offered blanket and pillow and lay down. In the darkness I stared at the ceiling, Presley's written words preying on my mind, a loose metal spring in the sofa pricking me in the back.

Amirul. A cousin and teacher called Elim. A compound: where?

Maskinia. That made everything fit. Did I want that?

Early the next morning I took my leave, after an uncomfortable cold wash and a cup of hot tea and a bun, my back sore from being prodded mercilessly during the night. Edwina was happy to be relieved of Presley's notebook, but at the door she put a hand on my arm.

—I won't get into trouble, Doc? For giving the man shelter?

—No, Edwina. If you're bothered, I'll speak up for you.

—Thank you.

When I got home, Joanie was tinkering in the kitchen.

—God, the mess you're in! Where were you?

—I have to take a shower.

We stood apart, staring at each other. It was impossible to move closer in the state I was.

—But where were you?

—To see a patient. The patient. He caught it badly, the Nostalgia worm . . . It was painful to watch.

—I'm sorry. Is he dead?

—Possibly. He was taken away.

She put a mug of coffee before me and for a while there was nothing more to say. On the television in the inside room *Good Morning America* was without an audience.

—Why get so involved with patients, Frank? What was special about him? You've aged in the process—in just a few weeks you've become pale and lost weight. You're tired and distracted. It's as if nothing else mattered to you. I don't matter to you.

—I couldn't help it, Joanie. There was something about him that I couldn't . . . I couldn't explain. Something that I'd never before felt with any other patient. It consumed me, this relationship. But you always matter to me, you know that. More than anything else.

At this confession, she smiled.

—Well, now you should rest. Don't go to work for a few days.

—I'll take it easy.

But I was on a roller coaster, I couldn't help but see this through—nor did I think it would let me go.

TWENTY-EIGHT

SITTING IN THE KITCHEN with a late breakfast, watching the snowflakes sticking to the bare branches outside, or descending lightly upon the grass—so beautiful, all this, the white and the green and the air itself shimmering in the sun—reason enough for life to go on. Ephemeral? Illusion, as Radha's god Krishna on his chariot would put it? It's real if we call it real, I say. We can touch it, feel the glorious snowflakes melt on our cheeks. If it's a dream, let's remain in the dream . . .

Such were my thoughts after Joanie had left for the day.

Then why didn't I feel I belonged anymore?

I was normally a positive sort, an optimist who valued life. It could only get better, I had always believed. I had implanted new memories in people, given them pasts they liked and sent them off to live longer and happier. But my experience on Walnut Street the previous night had shaken me out of myself. All this glorious natural beauty that I admired seemed not for me. More than that, my beloved Joanie was not for me.

Earlier after Joanie tucked me into bed, as my eyes closed with relief, the sight of her and the smell of her suffused into my mind and my dreams, nothing else seemed to matter, I was back in bliss and the night's experience was only a nightmare, Walnut Street on another planet that I need not see again. Presley was gone and would soon be forgotten, data in an archive, blown up into a zillion bits. But now that I was wide awake, it was this brightness around me that seemed the illusion, another world. And Presley was real, the agony of his breakdown clear in my mind as he lay on the steps at the bottom of the stage inside the church. The utterings from his mouth that suddenly turned him into a stranger to his friends, but not to me. A language I felt instinctively I should remember and understand but didn't. The key was missing.

His notebook burned in my pocket. Give it to the doc, he'd said to Edwina.

My name is Amirul. I had a cousin and teacher called Elim. I lived in a compound ...

And the compound was in Maskinia. There was another cousin, named Eduardo. And more ... Broken fragments like loose threads connecting our lives, taking us back ... there.

He and I and Holly Chu . . . that could be a line from a song.

I walked up to the river, sat down, stared longingly at its placidity, its seeming permanence. What stories it could tell. On the paved path, a group of people jogging, a bobbing bunch of bright colours. A woman pushing a stroller bent forward to talk sweet nothings to her child. Did I have to yield space to this newborn, or was there room for us both, for everyone?

Why go to other worlds when there's all this here, my mother the nature-lover would tell me . . .

I recall walking with her in the woods outside our home. It's cool in the morning and there's a mist hovering over the ground; momentarily the mist breaks and a burst of warm sunshine pours in. She stops and looks up in delight. She laughs. *Isn't it beautiful, isn't it beautiful! It is, Mom.* Her love of the *earth*, and of the wildflowers and trees and animals is awesome. I watch her spellbound. She's in a long skirt and a wide hat, I'm in jeans and long-sleeved shirt, and also wear a hat. She stoops to pick a purple lupine cluster from a bush and recites to it lines from William Blake, *Tyger, Tyger, burning bright In the forests of the night, What immortal hand or eye Could frame thy fearful symmetry?*

Rose, Mother, you must have been real, I whispered . . . as real as the mother who went by just now pushing the stroller . . . You *must* be real to save me . . .

Back home, Radha's face on the screen. Her full cheeks, smiling mouth, smooth forehead. How could she stay cheerful all the time—by assuming everything was an illusion?

—I need help, can you help me, Radha?

—I will help you. If you'll let me.

It's of dubious comfort, telling a happy person about your misery. By that unstudied law of conservation, your misery only increases her happiness. But Radha followed a different law. She generated happiness, radiated it like the sun.

—I feel eviscerated, Radha. I feel I'm evaporating.

—Let me help you, said Radha.

An hour later, on Masjid Road, off Rosecliffe Park Drive, a long line of men and boys in white long shirts and caps were quietly headed towards the mosque, as they'd been doing throughout the world through the centuries. For them space-time had shrunk to this point. It was Friday. This was another part of the city I'd never seen before. Rosecliffe Park was Radha's neck of woods, and it was here that she had suggested we meet. Why couldn't we meet elsewhere? At our café rendezvous? She said she wanted me to see another Toronto, watch people other than those I was used to.—You should see the rest of the world, Frank, she admonished gently.

We met at the intersection and, passing the mosque, which was a large, pale-coloured boxlike building of brick, we walked over to a strip mall at the dead end of Masjid Road and sat down for lunch at a crowded restaurant called Iqbal. We both chose vegetarian, but when it arrived I found it too strong and only had the flatbread.

Afterwards, as we had our tea, she said,—What's the matter, Frank? You are normally so calm and sure of yourself.

—I was feeling a bit blue when I called. I'm all right now. Perhaps seeing you has calmed me after all.

—That's nice. I'm your mood-lifter. The doctor's medicine.

—The doctor's doctor.

She was pleased and we said nothing for a while, mulling in silence. In her presence was comfort, security; I felt at ease with myself—though I was not sure *myself* had any meaning any longer, I did feel spontaneous and happier.

Much of the restaurant had emptied, and a girl came along with a trolley to clear the tables.

Radha was watching me intently, and I noticed for the first time the two dimples on her cheeks, and a blush, and I thought, Who are you? Where did you come from, where were you all this time; why didn't I know you before?

—Yes? she asked, and I repeated my thoughts loud enough for the girl with the trolley to look back at us.

Radha gave a laugh.—I was born in Vancouver, my grandparents were of Indian descent. I mean, *really*.

—How do you know?

—I saw my grandpa die, and later I sat with my father as he died. They gave him morphine, and I watched him give up his last breath. Is that real enough?

—I'm sorry.

—Why, Frank? I feel fortunate. We all must die. I have a bond with them, even though they are dead, and with my mother, who's alive. Tell me—she leaned forward,—have you seen a person die?

I shook my head. Presley, almost, perhaps. But I was in

the life business. I gave the promise of endless life. *We all must die?* That's not the way the world was going.

—I see. She turned pensive.—And you, Frank? Who are *you?*

—I was born in the Yukon, I began my litany.—I had wonderful parents, especially my mother . . . she was a poet who loved nature. She would speak of the *earth*. My father loved the stars. So I've believed, anyway, but it's only my fiction. And it makes me sad because I so desperately want it to be true. But I know I have no connections. There's no one in Yukon or anywhere else for me, there never was.

—You're a lonely man.

—I'm a lonely man.

She reached out for my hand.—I'm sorry. I shouldn't have said that.

—But it's true. All of us with extended lives—rejuvies as you call us—are truly lonely people.

—Tell me what's happening to you, Frank. Please tell me.

—It's just that. Suddenly I feel disconnected. Until now it didn't matter. I had my work, and Joanie, my girlfriend. I believed—still believe—in science and reason and progress. I live a privileged life and I am respected by my colleagues. I've received honours. I've made people feel more contented— removed misery—bad, unbearable memories . . .

—That's good, Frank. But—?

—But now I have this strange feeling that I myself don't belong . . . The world is not mine anymore. I who implanted idyllic fictions am a fiction myself and that fiction is falling apart.

—This morning when you called?

I nodded.

—Did you feel like ending your life, Frank?

—Perhaps I have had *enough*, as the young protester said the other day . . . I'm a fake. I'm a fiction. A character in a book.

—You're not a fake, Frank. You're real and you've done people good. Let me show you around, Frank. I want to show you something . . . something amazing and different from all your science and reason. I want to show you *unreason*. Magic. Come, let's go for a walk. You'll feel better afterwards.

We went out and walked up Masjid Road to the intersection where I had stood about an hour before, waiting and feeling lost as long-shirted men and boys in caps walked past me on their way to the mosque. Now, on the opposite side from us I saw something that in my alienation I had completely missed: a plain white wall standing some two metres inside the curb and in which, exactly at the corner, was an arched gate. Above it was a small but ornate sign that said, The Mall of the Spirit. Welcome.

—Have you been here before? Radha asked with a wondering smile. The question was rhetorical.

—No. But I heard about it, when it opened.

It's been called by our cultural gurus a spiritual wonderland, and a god fair, by implication vulgar and kitschy. But today I was open, in sense and mind, to receive new experiences, and come what may.

Dozens of people walked with us through the gate. It was Friday, this was where they came to put an end to their long work week. As we entered, I beheld a spectacular sight—tall fantastic structures linked by paths, each proclaiming in its unique architecture a sense of beauty and a brand of happiness, worship, and everlasting life. At the centre was an elaborate garden surrounding a small lake. We walked along for a while, past buildings with names like Durka Temple, Our Lady of Guadeloupe, Shango of the Thunder, Shining Buddha of the New Lotus, and Nizamuddin Overseas, listening to a twanging drone, a bass drumming, fragments of a speech, and lastly a throaty male chorus sung to a wailing string, before we arrived at what Radha called the pièce de résistance. It was a pyramid of a very light blue colour, rising two-thirds of the way up before being crowned by a structure with the shape of an open flower, the actual shrine, with a red pennant flying at its top. Along the sides of the pyramid were steps.

—Let's go up, shall we? Radha said with a laugh.—Do you have the stamina to climb?

—Right to the top? Why not?

—Come along.

The path, protected against the weather by a glass cover, had been laid out in such a deliberate manner as to render the walk long and arduous, winding up and down and at times staying level, with periodic stops along the way to sit and catch breath. There was a thin stream of people climbing up with purpose, and a few kids were running about for whom the occasion was evidently one of play.

From these heights the entire city lay exposed as though cut open neatly by a surgeon: downtown in the distance, the World Peace Tower shooting up; from there the roads leading north, pausing at the tall towers of the Centres of Enterprise, before proceeding finally to melt into the haze where lay the winding highways and endless suburbia. From our vantage point, the Mall of the Spirit was an island in the middle of a suburb, skirted by its white wall and a road going around.

We arrived at a station where flowers and sweets could be purchased to offer at the shrine and chai was served. This was the gathering place before the final stretch and it was crowded. There were people from Miami and Los Angeles, Nairobi and New Delhi, feeling good and exchanging pleasantries. The last climb was twenty steps straight and steeply up and packed with worshippers. Squeezed within this soft human mass slowly nudging forward, patiently grabbing every possible inch, and breathing the stale air of perfumed exhalations, I felt an uncanny, unknown sense of exhilaration. It seemed to me that I was regaining what I had lost and missed. Is this what it was like to *belong*? Is this what I'd come from, somewhere in the past? There was not an anxious face to see, only expectation and joy. Oh, but to believe! Periodically Radha turned to flash a smile at me. Her face was flushed and damp, her yellow sari dishevelled. We reached, almost stumbled, to the top where for a moment a cold hard breeze greeted us. Following her example I hit a bell hanging from a lintel and crossed the threshold into a dark and cool room. To our left an ancient-looking stone platform was lit by oil lamps, behind which in a niche sat a small black icon that looked like a shapeless lump.

—It is the goddess Kali, Radha whispered.—The statue is two thousand years old.

Beside the stage stood a bare-chested attendant, wearing a white wraparound below the waist. An overhead electric heater spread a warm glow upon the scene. Following my companion I joined hands, received a small powdery sweet with blessings in exchange for my offering, and departed through the exit doorway. Going down was not crowded. When we reached the base, we rested on a bench.

—I thought you worshipped Krishna, I said to Radha.

—That was Kali.

—But they are all the *same*, she replied.—That's why all life is connected, don't you see?

I looked blankly at her, and she laughed.

We resumed walking and immediately came upon a domed structure, a mosque. The outside was impressive, dazzling, the surface covered with minutely detailed geometric designs in blue, green, and gold that looked like inlays in stone. It turned out, as a plaque outside proudly explained, that the artwork had been produced optically, and was periodically replaced. The creator of the current display was one Shabaanu Robert Patel. Inside the building was a large hall with a forest of carved pillars, distributed evenly in a square array in what seemed to my mind a Cartesian simulation of infinity. A few people were on the carpet floor, praying as though to this mathematics, bowing and kneeling. The pillars too were optical, reaching up to another intricate geometry on the ceiling. I lingered, mesmerized by the repetitions.

—Does it do something to you? Radha whispered.—Do you feel like kneeling and praying to a higher being?

—It does feel strangely compelling, an homage to illusion. Or mystery. I don't know what I would pray to, or even how.

We came out into the garden. It was colder and getting dark, though the glowing prayer halls and shrines and the lampposts on the paths provided sufficient illumination. People walked on the track around the garden for their exercise, others sat in the heated alcoves designed to beat winter outdoors. Kids played.

I am a rational, modern man. I believe in the physical universe and its laws . , , they constitute my faith, and the great minds of the past are my prophets and gods; it's with them that I commune. I believe in the life and intelligence that has emerged from this universe, and in its continuity. You could call me a high priest of this materialist faith.

Such were my thoughts as we went out through the gate, but I did not say them aloud. I had been provoked. I had been impressed and humbled. Like an ancient sage Radha had taken me through a wonderland to show me alternative ways of perceiving the world. I acknowledged them, but did not quite understand them.

TWENTY-NINE

THAT EVENING JOANIE WENT OUT with the Friend. She was dressed up in tight-fitting jeans, black blouse, and stiletto heels she never wore with me. An enticing perfume, the heady citric scent of La Divina. All for him? She gave me a kiss before she stepped out, and as she left a look passed between us that said I must forget that I knew the man, the somewhat hysterical young man called Musa, who had called me *the elderly elite*, and she must forget that I knew and had forgotten him. Then we could continue our life together. I wished desperately to ask her, Do you stay with me only for the security? for a price? Isn't there some love you feel for me? A love I come back home to, a love I drink to at the admittedly elite Brick Club? Of course there was. Of course there was. A qualified love.

Roboserve brought me my scotch and sandwich.

I tried Radha. Her radiant face came up, once more to warm the heart.

—You look forlorn—are you alone?

—Yes, I'm afraid so.

—Where's Joanie gone?

—Out, with a friend.

—Oh. A pause. A searching look, wistful almost, then she said,—I wish I could come and keep you company.

In reply, I teased,—You didn't take me to your home when I was there—in Rosecliffe Park.

—There was no time, Frank. Next time. Also, to be completely honest, my mother is with me. She's handicapped and awkward with guests.

—Well, see you again. Bye.

—Bye . . . but give me a call any time and come over, Frank. I do mean it.

—Thanks, I will.

The evening news was on, arriving with the insistency of a bludgeon, the soundtrack loud and pulsing. Something had happened. It always happens, of course. News breaks all the time. Here's how it broke for me that night.

There had been a successful rescue of the hostages in Maskinia, carried out by a Northern Alliance special force. All the hostages were now safe and unharmed, except for two who had died in crossfire. Holly Chu was shot dead in an exchange. Details of the heroic mission followed.

The hostages had been held somewhere inside the

intricate maze of tunnels under the hills adjacent to the Warriors' compound. (An aerial view of the area showed the spot, marked by a pennant.) The maze had two secret exits (shown with flashing arrows); once these exits and the exact location of the prison became known, having been determined through informers, the special force dropped down from the air in the cover of dark, entered the tunnels, released the prisoners, and stormed the compound.

The entire rescue episode was reconstructed and played over so that we could share the experience as it happened— land with the forces and, following instructions, enter the Warriors' compound and join the fight and rescue. The unwary enemy patrols were shot down with homing darts. The tunnel system was entered easily through the two marked back entrances, from where we negotiated our way into the maze following a well-lit crooked path and arrived at the prison. The men were in one room, the women and children in another, all ragged and dazed. The four kids were quickly tranquilized, after which they and the frightened, dishevelled older hostages were all brought out and raced off towards two hovering helicopters. Two hostages were shot here. A Karukori jumped out of a chopper and raced to the rescue but was destroyed, its metallic guts spilling out. Another Karukori managed to scoop up the remains and return. The two choppers took off. A battle took place then, between us and the Warriors. All the terrorist soldiers present were killed, and one of ours. Holly Chu and a group of women, all carrying automatics, confronted us and we mowed them down. The terrorist compound was destroyed. In a fortified room, we found the chief of the terrorists, in his robe and cap, seated on a chair and guarded by three of his men. All were shot down, their faces blown off.

I came to with an excruciating pain in my right ankle, my heart was racing frantically, and I was on the ground and there was a whiff of perfume in my nose.

Joanie was kneeling before me and handed me a drink, which was tea with brandy.

—What happened, Frank?

—What happened . . . I don't know. Passed out, I guess. My head hurts . . . my ankle hurts . . . I was sitting on the sofa and suddenly—here I am on the ground. What's happening to me . . .

—I told you, you've been under stress.

Nothing was broken or out of sorts. I took a painkiller and we sat down to watch a repeat of the special report.

There were no estimates of the total casualties. The rescue commander was interviewed and congratulated, as was one of the Karukoris, as were the hostages upon their heroic welcome back home. The hostages would meet the president and the prime minister separately tomorrow.

Joanie helped me up and I hobbled with her to the kitchen table.

—What did you eat? I asked her.

—Roast beef. But I brought you a dessert.

I squeezed her hand.

—You still have fever. Let's go to bed.

———

I was wide awake before sunup with a distinct sense of having talked myself hoarse during the night, but Joanie was deep in the peaceful slumber, as they say, of the innocent. Facing up, breathing deeply—how beautifully white and tender that undulating belly—snoring lightly. I resisted the temptation to wake her with a kiss . . . on the eyes, the lips, the belly, the crotch. I recalled shouting and screaming. I had dreamed about the news last night. I got up and went to the living room, the tube turned on. Bill Goode's image dropped instantly on my kilim and he'd just turned around, having said something funny, and flashed his trademark grin as the audience applauded. The temptation was to punch that square block of a face. What had overcome me?

—So all's well that ends well and we have peace at last— for a few years at least, until someone in Barbaria wakes up from the dead. Or should we simply have nuked them?

Universal applause.

The special report on the rescue began again and I switched it off and went to my study.

FRANK: *Can you find references to these two people— Elim and Amirul—in Maskinia? Anything and everything about them.*

TOM: *There's a temporary embargo on any access to Maskinia. Sorry, Frank.*

Did I imagine that his tone sounded different, more brisk than usual?

Holly Chu's Profile no longer existed.

THIRTY

The Notebook

#54

The Journalist

In the late afternoon, on some days, Holly would go with Layela and Miriam and other women to the Warriors' compound and join others as they sat on the ground before their leader, Nkosi. The gathering would have been preannounced. The ground had been cleared and swept and sprinkled with lightly perfumed water. The sun was low, the shadows were long, and the heat wave of earlier that day was memory. There was the occasional burst of quick breeze. A relaxed and festive mood came to prevail. A man would come around with a long copper urn and serve coffee in little cups to all those gathered. Sweets, if anyone had cared to bring them, would go around, bits of peanut, sesame, or coconut brittle, or even candies. Nkosi, the title meaning lion, as Holly had discovered, would be sitting on his chair with its tall back and give homilies to the followers and answer questions. World news would always be discussed, one young man first standing up to summarize the latest. The women might sing or a man recite something. A couple might come forward to get formally engaged or a child blessed.

During one such session the Nkosi made it a point to praise the new member of their group, *the guest*, for her commitment and how well she had settled among them.

The hostages had been housed in the underground apartments, and Holly, now calling herself Umoja, had a few times explained the Warriors' cause and made the ransom demands in the broadcasts that were flashed across the globe. Regularly she had gone to visit the hostages to calm them. By now they no longer wished to tear off her hair, their torrents of abuse had eased. Whatever she had become, she was still one of them.

Nkosi, having praised her to the meeting, now asked her if she had any questions or concerns about her life as a Warrior. Was there anything that troubled her? Anything she did not understand about their cause?

—Be honest, don't be afraid. It is through criticism that we learn and progress. Other eyes are the best mirror for us to see ourselves honestly.

Encouraged, Holly said yes, there was something that troubled her.—Nkosi, forgive me, but doesn't it look immoral, capturing innocent men and women? Terrifying people who've done nothing themselves, and know no better, except what their government and media have told them? Isn't it cruel not allowing them to speak to their loved ones?

Nkosi smiled benignly through his white woolly beard; his cheeks were flushed, his eyes twinkled. He raised his hand partially and did a brief flicker with the fingers before replacing it on his lap. Then he answered her in his dry, crackly voice with its seductive charm and humour. He rarely raised his voice, and then only slightly. He never hurried.

—Haali, when they drop bombs on us, don't they terrify us, and kill the elderly and the women and children? When you count the number of ours dead and theirs, which is greater by far? Our hundred to their precious one. Do we not count because we are less fat and consume less and weigh less? When they live so much better than us, why do they come to grow their food on our lands? Why do they mistreat us? Who is responsible for that dead reactor that's bleeding poison into our water after forty years? Every time you see a boy with a shrivelled penis or a woman with four fingers, think of them. These hostages are our currency. With them we will buy back our people whom they hold prisoners. We will buy food and arms to protect us. Yes ... Where you come from, Haali, there is security and there is food. There is water. It is our people's dream of heaven. Here is desert and jungle and city filth. You come with a gun that sees far and you do not see the kill; the lion must use stealth using only his claws, and he looks at death face to face. He learns to come out at night.

Nkosi fell into contemplation, his beads rattling in his other hand, the wan smile still fixed on his smooth brown and hard face.

—Thank you, Nkosi, Holly said.

But why do you include me with *them;* am I still one of *them* to you? Am I still a *guest?* Am I not called Umoja now? I guess it will take time for you to completely accept me. But how long will you keep fighting? When will the conditions here improve? What do the children whom you bless look forward to except also to fight? And the women—they breed bastards and your strongmen do with them what they will.

All in the compound watched in silence their old leader sitting in contemplation and the foreign girl with the Chinese face looking down in embarrassment. It was some time before Nkosi spoke again. He did not look at her and sounded distant and dreamy.

—It is good you have spoken your mind, Haali. There is some truth to what you say. We should keep talking. We all have much to learn.

There was a story about the past that Holly had recently learned.

Long ago, there were three princes among the Warriors. The previous Nkosi, a wise and beloved leader, had two sons by two wives. The older one was called Elim, and his half-brother was Eduardo. Elim was tall and fair-skinned, his mother being white and American, and he was loved and respected in the compound. People still remembered him as the one who wore glasses and always had books in his hand. He was sent abroad to be educated and returned as a doctor. Eduardo, the dark one, though younger, was on the Warriors' Council of Seven and adviser to his father. Elim and Eduardo had a cousin called Amirul. He was shorter but handsome and had a thick crop of hair; he was a dashing fellow and liked to dress up; he was also volatile in nature and easily picked a fight. His uncle gave him a command in the militia, and he strutted about with a pistol at his belt. But he loved and worshipped his cousin Elim.

And so Eduardo, the youngest of the three, was the heir; Elim, the eldest, was the doctor, teacher, and intellectual; and Amirul was the fighter. Amirul was the hero who went on secret missions, and he brought back presents—clothes, perfumes, electronics—and stories about foreign shores. For Elim, who had lived abroad and returned to serve and who read everything, he brought books. On one mission, however, Amirul was captured and taken away, and that caused a great deal of grief in the compound. He had left behind his wife and little daughter. A few years after his capture, the Warriors themselves captured a foreign diplomat in Kenya, and as a part of the ransom the Warriors demanded Amirul's immediate release. Elim was sent to Europe to negotiate the release. However, the Alliance forces managed to rescue their diplomat meanwhile, and neither Amirul nor Elim were heard from again.

—You see, Haali, Nkosi said,—the war goes on. They do this to us, and we do that in reply.

He paused once more before going on, his voice tightening a little this time.

—We are small but not insignificant. We have ancient cultures ... and books ... they are stored in the tunnels. We are weak but we have our ways to fight back. After all, a mere fly can torment an elephant, until the elephant gives up and goes away.

—I understand, Nkosi, said Holly-Umoja. And her question *But for how long?* had no answer.

#55

The Gentle Warrior

Pres, I see you. Stiff and straight as a mummy, staring up right into the powerful white glare of lights exposing you. Men and women all around you, a doctor in white coat and a nurse in white, in a white room, all eyes shifting from the overhead screens to your open head. Still but not dead, now only part of an electric circuit, sending signals into those very probes that you dreaded so much.

Where, what, who. Where, Amirul, where ...?

And you tell them—your brain tells them. From the deep recesses of memory, it leaks out the information. The tunnels of Maskinia.

THIRTY-ONE

—PRESLEY SMITH DIED PEACEFULLY, Joe Green assured me sympathetically.

I hadn't asked him for this news, though admittedly Presley had been on my mind constantly since I last saw him being wheeled away to the ambulance. I did not think he would survive his condition, so the news didn't surprise me.

Joe's office, high up in the Vega Tower, overlooked Freedom Park, a grey barren wintry space at present, but the convertible window could look out over any scene in the universe. It showed now a botanical garden in full bloom, oblivious of the season and that the ground was sixty floors below. The furniture was solid but sleek, the chairs comfortable. I was here because this time I had been summoned, though not in that language. Joe's message said that Presley

Smith had died in the Department's care and would I like to come over and discuss his case; there were some loose ends to sort. It is rare that I find myself on the other side of the desk this way, and it was not an easy position.

—He could have died peacefully anywhere, Joe, I replied.

What I meant to say was that there was no need to hound him or snatch him away in his last hours. How easy it was for this practiced bureaucrat to ignore the fact that he himself had put out a wanted call for Presley, thus running him underground. And what did *peacefully* mean? I had watched the man in agony, his memory disintegrating. A brain boiling out its contents. That harrowing scene inside the Holy Trinity Church remains indelible on my mind.

We didn't let him suffer, Joe explained.—He died under medication. If he had come to us sooner, we could have saved him, Dr Sina. Frankly—he paused, becoming aware of the pun,—I don't know why he went to such lengths to avoid us.

—He was afraid of being turned into yet someone else— the way your window there creates another view.

The window had altered to look over a blue and green horizon, an endlessly bland emptiness. If it had a mood sensor, it must have been off.

I should have been on my guard, yet rather carelessly I had let my feelings show. I had implicitly confessed to having been in contact with Presley while he was in hiding, and therefore assisting him in his evasion and lying to the Department when questioned about him. Acted illegally. Presley became more than a patient for me. But of course Joe Green knew all that already.

He said, unfazed,—That might not have been necessary. Though if it were needed to save his life, what's wrong with that? Life goes on, improved, you discard the old model. It's forgotten and gone. *You* know that, if anyone does.

—Yes, I do. I've preached that often enough. But Presley wanted to cure himself. Or die as himself, if he must. Or didn't he have a choice? He was your man, as you said?

Joe stared blankly at me, said in a flat voice,—Certainly. And the patient doesn't know what's best.

He looked up quickly over my head. There was a shuffle behind me, from where now a mellifluous voice intoned,

—All that is academic. Obviously you know by now, Frank, that Presley was a terrorist in his previous life. More precisely, he was a military commander in the Warriors of Freedom in Maskinia. It was called something else then— the Warriors of Justice or something grand like that. Do you recall that, Frank?

I'd turned around and was gawking at the man who had introduced himself as Arthur Axe the other day at my lecture, but who I had felt certain even then was Author X of DIS. He had on a plaid jacket, solid blue shirt, and dull red tie. His deep forehead glistened, and his loose posture, as he softly walked in, was that of someone who's never in a hurry.

He bore a beatific smile as he headed for the straight-backed chair to my left, continuing, as matter-of-fact as you would have it,—Regardless of his record, when Amirul was captured—that was Presley's previous name—he was given a chance at another life. That's an example of the good-will and grace of our civilization—which is generous and progressive. But our present governments, I would inform you, are not as kindly disposed to our liberal approach to rehabilitating terrorists. I'm Arthur, by the way.

His eyes closed on mine as we shook hands. His hand was limp; evidently his strengths were inner.

Arthur Axe, the author of Presley's life and, as I now know, mine also. The one whose presence once more sent a chill through me. A chill of, yes, terror. His friendly exterior was as false as perhaps his name. He knew more about me than I did, this powerful man who had imagined my tender-hearted poetic mother and my astronomer father in Yukon and given them a place in my life. Who put Blake and Rumi in her head and named a distant planet after him. Should I be thankful to him for having given me those positive influences? Those touching and wonderful memories? Perhaps they were based on real ones, from my life? How many creatures like me did he know, inside out? How many destinies had he created, and watched, as they unfolded?

—We spoke at your lecture. I asked a question, he reminded me.

—Of course, I remember.

—A very interesting lecture, Frank. It has a lot of bearing on what we do here. We have actually used some of your keen observations and theories in our mission here.

—That's very flattering . . . Joe has also told me that. Thank you. You said Presley had been a terrorist . . .

And what was I? But I didn't ask him that.

—Yes. He was captured while on a mission, interrogated, then went on to become a useful citizen, assimilated into our society, with a new past and bearing no harm to anybody. He could have gone back to that.

—A benign nobody. A laughable, variegated man . . . a lonely man.

Spoken perhaps too forcefully. I could have said more: Did you have to turn him into a parody, a joke, merely for your own pleasure?

—Better than execution, he replied.—Or a long prison sentence on an island somewhere. What kind of a man is he then? Don't let your liberal sympathies get the better of you, Frank. There are necessities.

What kind of choice had Amirul been given, I couldn't help thinking. Did he himself ask for another life? What state was he in, after the *advanced* interrogation, as the jargon has it? Why had they wanted him back so desperately?

—A penny for your thoughts, Frank.

I shook my head.—I'm not convinced the man Amirul would have asked for a new, benign life. He would have been the sort of personality that would want to hold on to his beliefs—to die for them.

—A fanatic, Joe Green said knowingly, with a look at Axe.

—They exist.

Radha had told me there were people who could recall and dwell into their previous existences. Her sort of past avatars are different from ours, the mind doctors', but when the other day I saw on television the rescue operation at the compound in Maskinia, I knew I had seen the place, I could recognize those hills where I would go for walks. And I saw my little brother's face blown off. Then I fainted, and Joanie revived me.

Author X was saying,—At the last stage, we also needed information from him, about the location of the hostages. All we wanted initially was to stitch up his memory. We were his guardians, for sure. The parents of his personality, if you will. His warranty was with us. But when the hostage crisis happened, the security forces needed details about the tunnels. The location of those exits was vital to the rescue. They had not been opened in decades, few people could know about them, let alone their exact location. But our patient did. Lives were saved.

—Didn't he reveal that information during his first interrogation—when he was captured? It would have been in the records, surely.

—That was a long time ago. What the interrogators extracted was partial—a case of negligence, we can say now. The sin of hubris. The tunnels were not deemed important at the time. They must have thought bombing would expose them anyway. It didn't. Those tunnels are deep and complicated.

I turned to Joe, who'd been quiet all this while.—You asked me to come here.

—Yes. We thought we should talk here this time. And Dr Axe wished to meet you in person.

—Here I am!

—Here you are. Dr Sina, how did Presley's intruder thoughts affect you? What did you make of them?

—I sympathized with him. And of course I found these stray thoughts intriguing . . . I was curious.

Arthur Axe jumped in:

—How so, Frank?

—I wondered what the lion meant; and there was the car with the red fender . . . and a little girl in the rain.

—And more?

—I think so, a couple, but I can't recall them now.

I'd said too much and for a moment he became thoughtful. Then he continued,—Would you mind recording them for us, Frank? In your words, how you remember them, in the order in which he revealed them to you?

—I'll do that.

—Thank you. What we would like to know is whether these thoughts caught on in you, started a process in you.

I had to lie.—Not much of a process, I'm afraid. They were a patient's thoughts and I found them intriguing. I puzzled over them for some time. But nothing more. They were like other curious thoughts that find a place in the mind temporarily but eventually fade away and are forgotten.

—Forgotten.

—Yes.

He didn't believe me. And I realized I'd just given him two of Presley's thoughts with one of mine.

—That's good. But I would like to see you in a month, Frank, and chat with you. Sooner if you so decide.

I could have asked why, but there was no sense going through a rigmarole. We all knew where we stood.

—I'll do that. Can I ask you something, though?

—Go ahead, Frank.

—Why did you give him the name Presley?

Joe smiled, but the older man's look only softened and he spoke slowly,—In the interrogation process at that time, they liked to play Elvis Presley songs ... among others. He could have been called Ringo Smith.

As I got up to go, Arthur Axe asked,—And Frank, what did you make of that reporter Holly Chu's defection in Maskinia? Quite a coincidence, eh? You followed the case?

The look he gave me said, We know a lot more than you think.

—Yes, I've followed it. A strange case—and sad. Misguided youth, surely. Stockholm syndrome, they say. A life wasted.

—Yes.

THIRTY-TWO

NEITHER OF US MENTIONED JOANIE.

Musa Abbas is an unemployed young physicist, like me a graduate of the Parallax. That came as a large surprise. There was even more in common between us—he'd worked with brains, he said. His last job was at a space colony studying the effects of weightlessness on the quantum circuits inside small animal brains. He even arrived at a theoretical model to explain the results.

—And? I asked, impressed.

—Nothing. The project was considered of minor importance and shelved. For the time being. Someone else will probably be given it and take it forward. The progress of science. But I wanted to return anyway.

He looked away; he'd rather have talked of something else. His hostility had not gone away, it was simply on hold for the moment. Our meeting at the Brick was at my request. I wanted to find out what he was like. I was the inquisitive elder. And he was not the anarchist I had taken him for, just an angry young man without a job. A bright one. On his subject he could go on forever, as I could on mine.

Our food arrived.

—The good thing about the fish here is that it is bred on the premises—the water is free of pollution.

—Not everybody can afford it, though.

—Yes. But for those of us who can, why not?

I sounded exactly like Joe Green. Was it so long ago in another life when I would have thought like Musa? I knew the arguments by heart. But that life was beyond me, even in memory.

The young man before me had few prospects. He had even less money. Jobs for the professional young are scarce, and in his case the science market happens to be in its saturated cycle. He didn't want to talk about prospects. Both parents are from West Asia, mother a beautician, father a man's stylist. They're real, and immigrants. He didn't expect much from them. He has siblings. He didn't want to talk about any of them either.

What could he offer Joanie to make her happy? What do the young need anyway, who are in love? And what do I know of such love, you might ask, and you would be right. But she's used to more, she wouldn't last with him the way he is. I've spoilt her. Would she eventually abandon me for him if he found better prospects? Now that I had seen and met him, the Friend, that question nagged.

—Dr Sina—I'm not sure why you wanted to meet me. I mean . . .

—Frank. Call me that. I hope I've not wasted your time. I thought I would like to see you again. The last time you had very strong views on what I should do with my life. Perhaps if you saw me as a fellow human and not a Frankenstein . . .

It never fails to surprise how personal contact can change preconceptions. At my lecture he'd been the rabble-rouser, calling me names and shouting at me. Now here he was, timid as could be.

—I . . . I didn't quite mean it like that. It was only a . . . a philosophical argument.

—Passionately stated.

—Yes. I'm sorry.

—No need. You believe it—maybe not in its passionate version. I smiled broadly.—And you gave me something to think about.

—If you say so.

We became quiet. He had ordered pomegranate juice and I, after a moment's hesitation, a Chablis.

—Tell me, what do you do for recreation—how do you pass time?

He looked up surprised.—I jog and play chess. I have enough time. I'm learning to play squash . . .

He broke off in embarrassment, and I didn't ask him who was teaching him the sport, what facilities he used, which of the three resident pros at the Brick trained him. Don't go with Salman, I would surely have advised. He's rough. But then you're young.

I'd already noticed that some of the waiters recognized the young man sitting in the booth across from me. He looked nervous. He must have known by now that I knew about Joanie and him. But we would not mention her, it was him and me.

—But my passion is poetry, he said.

—Really? My mother wrote poetry.

That didn't impress him. She was ancient.

—I write the poems first, and then I transmute them into different forms—video, multilingual, and musical—electronically. It's all abstract at the end . . . of interest to nobody but me . . . and a few friends.

I didn't know that Joanie was into that sort of thing.

—Could you send me something to listen to?

—Yes, I'd be delighted to!

That broke some ice, didn't it. I must have heard some of his music, I thought, probably the abstract stuff that she called modern. I had not liked it, but perhaps now with a context I might appreciate it.

—If you're looking for work, I can put in a word for you at the Sunflower. With your experience, they could use you.

—Dr Sina . . . Frank, I don't believe in the kind of work you do.

—You could do something technical. It's a tough market out there, as you've found out. A word in the right ear helped even Einstein.

—Let me think about it. Thank you.

We exchanged information.

I dropped him off at Yonge and Eglinton—no, he assured me, there was no protest scheduled today. I watched him lift his hood against the wind, square his shoulders, and stride off jauntily across the street. Watching him, the prospects of an entire life ahead of him, predicting the excitement of success to come despite the present uncertainty, could one blame oneself for envy, wanting to keep on, have as long a life as possible? But at what price—losing awareness of the very life you want to prolong. But Joanie—wasn't she worth the price?

Lovelys Café looked somewhat desolate this afternoon. There was only a silent, ragtag remnant of the religious protesters left. The display window had become a shrine, with a raised framed photograph of the martyr surrounded by heaps of flowers. Dr Kumar had become a god. There's no law against worship, I told myself, and I told the taxi to move on.

Lamar greeted me as I reached work.

—Look, Frank.

The Warhol Elvis was gone from its place on the partition. Instead there was a painting with three broad swaths of colour, white, black, and red. Such were the kinds of mind games they played, the overcultured folk at the Department. What was watching me now, in place of Elvis with the gun? With my knowledge, I was as dangerous as Presley had been and as much a risk to myself—but not as useful, now that the compound in Maskinia had been successfully raided. Dr Axe knew that. He'd given me time.

—What should I do with our Presley file, Frank? Shall I destroy it?

That's what we must do with discarded lives as clients move on. Shred them into electronic smithereens. But Presley died as Presley.

—We still have it?

—Why, yes!

—Let me look at it.

I entered my office and brought up the file. Presley Smith of Toronto, Ontario. Transcripts of our interviews, the lab results, my prescription. *Consultations terminated at client's request.* There was even included my chat with Joe Green. As my final entry, I now wrote, *Died as Presley Smith from Leaking Memory (Nostalgia) Syndrome, overstimulation of the nervous system. Former life: Amirul, of Maskinia. Military commander, The Freedom Warriors, captured by Alliance agents. Interrogated, transformed.*

That was it, complete. But we could not preserve it, and what was the point, anyway? DIS, of course, would already have its version.

—Okay, dump it, I told Lamar.

Goodbye, Amirul. I remember the books you brought for me.

Joanie handed me my drink and came to sit down on my armrest, put a hand on my shoulder and gave me a peck.

—Not watching the news today, Frank?

—No. It's broken enough for me, and it's broken all around me.

I gave her a grin that did not come out funny at all.

—You're in a strange mood. That's not like you at all. You've watched the news since as long as I've known you.

—But now I'm here all for you.

She wasn't convinced. She cozied up closer and we sat there like that, our bodies touching, almost breathing together, for a long while. I thought of my meeting with Musa, my interview at DIS, the life choice I had now determined to make. Through the wide window the night looked quietly mysterious, shaded yellow by the external lights, snow falling rapidly in globs, wrapping the tree branches coarsely in white. On the speakers, Beethoven's Ninth. Joy.

—Tell me, Joanie. If you had a choice to have anything you wanted, any lifestyle, anywhere, what would you have?

—That's not a real question.

—Would you pick a life with me, forever? The life we're leading now?

—That's too hypothetical. What's on your mind?

I thought about this, then said,—I'm sorry. That wasn't fair. I'm feeling insecure today, that's all.

She leaned forward, gently took my head in her hands, and looked into my eyes—ah, that scent of La Divina—and she said,—We are what we are, you and I. And I like you as you are. Isn't that enough?

—Of course it is.

—Anyway, what did you have in mind?

—I'm not sure anymore.

But a lie from you would have felt good.

———

—You planning to move on, Frank? Ali asked.—To what? You're doing all right with your life. It's I who should be moving on. Look at this—He made a sweeping gesture at the array of displays on his table.—Well?

—To better prospects.

Ali is my lawyer, with a trademark egg-shaped head he has refused to have remodelled, a few strands of hair freely scattered across the bald pate.

—And you want to leave her everything you've got? Is that wise, Frank? No, it's not. You can decide to take enough with you. You'll need it, for a soft, cushioned landing.

—I don't think I'll need it, Ali. Let her have the security to live as she wishes.

Ali didn't speak for some time, as he read from his pad. Finally he looked up.

—Here's what I suggest. I insist, Frank, or I'm not doing this. In the emotion of the moment people make decisions they often regret. We know that. I'm here to protect you. We'll stipulate that the transfer of assets be finalized only after the four-week grace period. If during that period in your new youthful life you apply for a review, which I'm sure you will when you try to buy a house and find a woman or something, then I as your trustee will adjust the transfer as per written instructions that I will help you draw up now.

By law a person who's moved on can be represented by a trustee for four weeks, in order to make the transition smoother. After that there are no adjustments. All records are destroyed.

—All right. But one week, Ali. Not four.

THIRTY-THREE

The Notebook

#56
The Doctor and Teacher
My name is Elim Angaza. I was a teacher and doctor in
Maskinia. My father, the chief, of whom I was very fond,
was a tall and sturdy man, an imposing figure with a high
forehead and a small goatee. As chief, he was addressed as
Nkosi. He was a wise man. He had three wives, one of whom
was my mother, Selma, from Boston, and several children.
He told me once that there were different approaches in the
struggle for human dignity, and that mine was the path
of the intellect, or education. I would not be asked to fight
because he knew I was repelled by violence of any kind. He

sent me to college in Boston. There I studied mathematics, which I loved very much, but later I decided to attend medical school. By this time my mother had also returned to Boston with my little sister. I was devoted to her and we spent a lot of time together. I remember in particular going to concerts with her. I returned to Maskinia because there were no doctors left there and my father called. I was to run the local hospital and was also put in charge of a school. The school building consisted of two rooms with writing boards and desks and chairs. It was some distance away from the compound, which could be attacked by air. With the aid of two young assistants I taught the young ones language and mathematics, and everything else about the world. It was not easy, because our mission was to fight, and all our rhetoric was about justice and vengeance. All the boys wanted to become fighters. My half-brother, Eduardo, was younger than me; he was the dark one and was my father's political adviser. It was acknowledged that he would be the next Nkosi. We had a cousin, Amirul, a military commander much admired and worshipped by the youth. Women adored him. He was also volatile in nature and easily picked a fight. My father gave him a command in the militia, and he strutted about with a pistol at his belt. But he loved and respected me. He often went on missions abroad and brought back presents. Mine were always books and music. One title I can recall was Tolstoy's *War and Peace*. He also brought back medicines. One day, news came that Amirul had been captured in Rome. It was received with shock and grief in the compound; for many months nothing was heard from or about him and it was presumed that he was dead. And then about a year after his capture, my father and my brother Eduardo called me one morning from school and advised me that there was news of Amirul. He was alive. Our fighters had captured some diplomat in Libya, and it was proposed we exchange him for Amirul. This had been agreed in principle. My father asked me, since I had been educated in the north, and specifically in Boston, where I had a sister and cousins on my mother's side, to go with a small team to negotiate the exchange. I flew to Tripoli from Nairobi. The same morning as I arrived, as I came out of the hotel and was waiting for a taxi, a van drew up and I was shoved by three men into it.

THIRTY-FOUR

—WHAT ARE YOU SAYING, FRANK?

We had come to meet at Iqbal Restaurant in Rosecliffe Park, Radha and I, and I was feeling joyously unburdened. It was not the local chai that brought on this euphoria— though I would never have thought that the sweet, cloying tea with the scent of Eastern spices would come to suit my taste, which has leaned towards the austere and straight; it was the accomplishments of the previous two days, satisfactorily shedding a life (and in the process benefiting two young people), that had done it. There remained a residual ache, but I shan't dwell on it.

I had done what was right. That sounds corny, as they say. Other, more clever adjectives come to mind. But it is only by pursuing this single-minded purpose that I've been able so far to thwart Frank Sina's complete unravelling—the evaporation into nothingness of Arthur Axe's creation. The destruction of his fiction. Into nothingness? Even a fiction has its impact, leaves an imprint—people might say there was Frank Sina, somewhat stern of visage, broody; he was an expert on Nostalgia and rejuvenation and performed creative memory implantations; he was Joan Wayne's unlikely lover, and disappeared perhaps into another life. As real as Tolstoy's Pierre Bezukhov.

Arthur Axe and I must both have been relatively young when I was transformed. And I ended up a specialist in the same field as his. As I've said before, irony is his strong suit. I wonder what his taste in literature is—or do only his own fictions interest him nowadays?

The creamy tea was strong and subtly spiked. On one wall, a television was turned to XBN, which was hectoring viewers with more news and analyses, but happily it was on mute.

In front of me, Radha had an anxious, wide-eyed look.

—You can't be serious, Frank.

—I am. I've decided I will not consume resources any longer, I will bequeath what I own and what I will potentially consume to the young ones. The Babies.

—You can't just die.

It is flattering to think that she will miss me.

—There's no death, remember? You yourself said that we simply change bodies, the soul is eternal.

—But that . . . that's not for you, Frank. And you don't believe in the soul.

—Who's talking now?

—I know you're joking.

—I'm not, Radha. I don't think I have a choice. I'm suffering from a certain malaise of the brain—the Nostalgia syndrome, as we call it—and my previous life is coming back to me and will soon overwhelm me in waves. It's as simple as that. So it's not all out of altruism. But I do feel good about whatever is happening. It's right.

Not as simple, of course. I needed a place where I could let it happen, a refuge with a friend . . . where I could expire with dignity, let that other life reclaim me. And where I could also complete this account of my recent experiences.

Radha is the only friend I have. Whatever she proclaims, deep in her heart she understands me.

—We can control it through yoga, Frank. And meditation.

She didn't ask me about my previous life, but then she's known me only as Frank Sina, the rejuvie doctor whom she likes. Regardless of her beliefs in karma and the cycles of life, she lives her life as if nothing else matters but the here and now. But for me there is something else, and it does matter.

—I don't want to control it, Radha. I want it all to come back to me. I want to know who I was—actually, who I was born as, who I really am. I want to recall my real family. I want to know my friends and relations even if they are now dead or unreachable to me. My brother, my cousin . . .

And a wife and a child, though I can hardly picture them yet, except the child peering through a sheet of rain. There's much that's trying to repossess me.

She was staring at me, trying to read me.

—What use is it anymore, Frank, if it's unreachable? All memory? You are here, and that's all that matters. Am I not real? And Joanie? And your patients? Don't we all matter?

What to say? Yes, but—?

She continued,—This is all there is for now, all this around you, you have to live it.

—There's a life I must reclaim, Radha . . . even briefly . . . even if it's in shreds, it's mine. And as a scientist I am also curious about it.

—What a funny thing to say. Were you a scientist there, in this other life you are talking about?

I couldn't help but grin at her.—Touché. Just being vain, I suppose, in this life . . . Maybe I was always vain.

—We'll see. Meanwhile you are here with me. You've left your home?

—And my work. I left a note for Joanie and her beau.

And the Department will be looking for me.

She was smiling.—You're a romantic, Frank.

She had a wedding ceremony to attend, which was why she was dressed up so gorgeously, and yes, she said, I must go with her. My suit would do, because for a man almost anything was all right at these occasions. Afterwards she would take me home and we would talk more about my plans.

When we departed, night had fallen and it was dark outside but for the dim light from the small supermarket next door still doing business.

———

The wedding was in a public hall decorated to look like the interior of a large and opulent marquee, with light arrangements, paper frills, and flowers. The floor was covered with a lush, red carpet. The chairs were all taken, and the remaining guests stood in groups at the back. Reedy ceremonial music screeched in the background, bouquets of sensual fragrances rode the air, their wearers looking brilliant and happy with excitement, oblivious of their partners, some of whom had broken loose to cluster around the drinks table like painted iron nails at a magnet. The noise was indescribable. Children ran about like dressed engines, screaming at the tops of their voices.

The groom arrived, dressed in white-and-gold long shirt and pants, a veil of white flowers covering his face, and went to sit on the stage beside the two priests in front of a small fire. The bride arrived, dressed in red and gold, decked in gold and diamonds, and was walked, leaning on her father, to sit next to the groom. The priest began a chant, and when he was finished, he tied the frilled hems of the couple's clothes together, and they walked around the fire.

—Seven times, whispered Radha next to me.—Seven times, according to Indian tradition.

—Aren't you from Vancouver? I whispered.

She slapped my arm, then gave it an affectionate squeeze.

After the ceremonies I was taken around and introduced to the bride and the groom, who turned out to be a nephew of the now famous demigod Professor Kumar. When I was introduced to the professor's wife, Anita, I couldn't help but utter my condolences, to which she came back sharply,

—Why? He's free, he's attained moksha.

—Salvation, Radha explained to me as we walked away, then added,—That means he's found eternal bliss and will not return.

—Thank God.

—He's now a god. They have applied for a space for him at the Mall of the Spirit.

It is this kind of unthinking certainty which modern science deplores. You are dangerous, we say. Knowledge must stand on empirical fact and logic. This is a man, we say. This is his brain, we explain. These its circuits and functions. Ergo, this is what he is. But is that all he is? Perhaps we do need the anarchic, irrational certainty of the likes of Anita Kumar and her husband, and the happy, contradictory philosophy of Radha, if only as an antidote against the smug certainty of my kind? Arthur Axe's kind. Any absolute certainty is tainted by its very nature. Is this Dr Frank Sina, ScD, opining or Elim Angaza, the country teacher from Maskinia?

We departed and walked along Rosecliffe Park Drive, past the Mall of the Spirit. Even at this late hour a fair number of people were paying their respects at their special places of worship. A string of red-and-yellow taxis stood idly in a ring round the island mall. A series of bright lights ran along atop its wall. The Kali temple twinkled high atop its pyramid, and the mosque was bathed in a soft blue glow, a rich, male sound emanating from its depths; there would be Mary with Child benignly blessing the restless world from her perch, and the god Shango with his thunderbolt. And all the various others.

—All these devout worshippers, I asked,—they would not like to be rejuvenated, to live longer?

—Most would if they could afford it. People are not consistent, as you know. They want everything. And rejuvenation is attractive.

She smiled. A bell gave a single distant peal high up at the temple, announcing a worshipper.

She lives in a townhouse with her mother, Sita, who greeted us happily at the door from her wheelchair. She spun around and led the way in, saying,—You're late, Radha. Did you eat?

—Yes, we ate, Mom. This is Frank. We took a stroll after the wedding. The Mall looks beautiful.

—It always does at night, doesn't it, especially when it's clear and cold as tonight. Now tell me about the wedding—how was it?

Radha described the wedding, naming all acquaintances who were present, what they wore, what food was served, what was said by whom. She went to the kitchen to make tea. Meanwhile I answered Sita's questions as discreetly as I could. I had problems at home, I told her, and Radha had kindly offered me space to spend a night or two, if Sita didn't mind. As her daughter laid out the green tea with biscuits, Sita described her life in Vancouver. Her husband had been a policeman who was shot in the streets two decades ago. She herself was a homemaker; she had two sons besides Radha.

There had been conflicts with her sons, so she followed Radha to Toronto.

The sensations of the past hours had numbed my own thoughts, but now I felt tired and somewhat depressed. I sensed Elim calling me from somewhere in a jungle of thoughts inside my brain. Sita stopped talking abruptly, said goodnight, and wheeled herself to her room on the ground floor. Radha showed me to the guest room upstairs, and I sat down on the single bed. Instead of leaving, however, she sat down on a chair at the bedside and put on a bright smile.

—Let's meditate together, she said enthusiastically.—We can be seated where we are.

—No, can I just be alone, I replied.—Do you mind?

—Will you be all right? Why don't I stay with you for a while?

—Thank you, but I will be all right. Thank you again. I will see you in the morning.

She stood up to leave, and on her way out paused at the door, and for that anxious look on my behalf I felt grateful. It was tempting to yield and let her administer to me, meditation and all the rigmarole. A cool hand on my forehead. But I'd had enough for today, I needed time to gather myself and prepare. Soon it would be time to call it quits. Time to enter that chaos and return to that tumultuous world that beckoned vaguely but persistently. It was mine, after all.

—Tell me, Frank, you're not serious. That you won't . . . that you'll at least let me try to help you . . . You'll call me.

I believe she was close to tears.

—But I thought you believed in such a step, Radha. There's no death, you've always said. You quoted your Krishna to me and . . . at Lovelys, remember?

She blushed. It was our first meeting and she had argued there was no such thing as death. That it was pointless to prolong life. *Don't you see, there is no such thing as death.*

—Krishna didn't say you don't live your life. Choosing to die is for people who are so advanced spiritually that they know when their time has come. They are not ordinary people.

I smiled at her.—I may not be advanced spiritually, but I know my time has come. I am not ordinary either. I have a past life and suffer from Nostalgia.

—I will help you.

In that interlude of silence now, I wondered what Joanie was doing in that house by the river; how lovely it was just to watch her when I returned from work, to hold her tenderly . . . we did make a home together. Perhaps she was at the club now with Musa. I thought of the fragments I'd recalled recently of my former life. I gazed at the woman at the door who made me feel so unfettered and released and loved; and whom, I thought, I had come to love too.

—I have to do it, Radha. I have to go home . . . You must let me, when the time comes. Be with me then, comfort me.

She nodded.—Okay. I'll pray for you. My mom and I and my friends will gather round you and pray so hard together it will be a deafening send-off!

I watched her leave and picked up my notebook and pencil.

THIRTY-FIVE

The Notebook

#57

The Bridegroom

On my wedding day I was not allowed to see Roxana. While I showered and was perfumed, and waited with the men, her male folks came around to banter, and to make certain I would not venture out with others to take a sneak peek at my bride. There was my father the Nkosi and my brother and my cousin. I wore a white collarless kurta brought by my mother from Boston. My sister had not come. As we sat there on the decorated front porch there came from the backyard kitchen the scent of fragrant rice pilau, and the smell of goat roasting and potatoes frying. From Roxana's end further up the street and outside the compound came the sound of women singing. Little girls went to and from our houses to report on the proceedings. The compound gates that day were left open. Finally a band was heard, tambourines and drums, and a trumpet, as the bridal procession approached, the women singing in a lilting chorus about the bride and the groom and the wedding night. She arrived at the door escorted by the women, her face pink with shyness, wearing a pure white robe with a red binding at the throat and a thin veil also brought by my mother; her hair was bedecked with jasmines, her hands and feet were hennaed. The music stopped, and we sat on the low stools and my father the Nkosi began to officiate. Her lips were full, her hair thick and wavy, we spent the most joyful time together possible . . .

On the day I left it was raining in sheets, Roxana and the baby Saida were on the porch waving.

THIRTY-SIX

ARTHUR AXE: *Well, Tom, here we are. Two more bite the dust.*

TOM: *Yes, Art. I feel for you—your two favourite fictions rejected.*

AXE: *It's more the technology, as we both know, that began to unwind. Though I get your point, both characters, Presley and Frank—I can hardly call him Dr Sina, can I?— both rejected the treatment that could have saved them.*

TOM: *The irony is, Art, that the doctor refused to heal himself.*

AXE: *The irony is, yes, Tom. Though I myself would call him an unstable fiction. An unviable character. I was young when we made him. Perhaps we put too much of himself into*

*the new fiction. Not always a good idea. As he himself could
have told us.*

TOM: *Yes, he could have, Art.*

AXE: *Mind you, they both lasted a long time; both were
called in and repaired, weren't they?*

TOM: *Sorry, that was before I myself was transitioned,
Art. But we have the records.*

AXE: *Well here we are, then, all transitioned. Nothing
wrong with us, is there?*

TOM: *Not that I can see, Art.*

. . .

AXE: *Now, Frank . . .*

TOM: *What about Frank, Art?*

AXE: *You would hardly call Frank a terrorist.*

TOM: *No, Art. Elim Angaza was a doctor and teacher.*

AXE: *Not just that. A Norbert Weiner Fellow in mathematics at MIT. What made him drop all that and return
home? What is home, after all? What a waste of talent, to take
it to wither away behind the Border. What would they know in
that hellhole about the beauties of science, mathematics, or art?*

TOM: *It makes you think.*

AXE: *It certainly does. We brought that talent back,
though. And it aided us. But he didn't know that—and that's
the irony, if you want one.*

TOM: *It certainly is. I can see that, Art.*

AXE: *Amirul, on the other hand . . .*

TOM: *Definitely dangerous.*

AXE: *Yes. Even transformed. Of all the practitioners
available, he sought out Frank Sina. And Frank Sina protected*

him. *Amirul knew exactly where he could find sympathy. The worm knew just where to go to survive. What do you say?*

TOM: *They were brothers, Art. And blood is—*

AXE: *Yes. Thicker than water. It's in those relationships that the worm hides . . .*

. . .

TOM: *You're thinking, Axe.*

AXE: *That's my job. There's much to ponder after this.*

TOM: *I can help you with that.*

AXE: *Tell me, Tom. What accuracy would you place in Frank's so-called entries in his Notebook? His feats of imagination. Always dangerous, flights of imagination, no telling where they might take one. How much truth do they contain? How much of Holly Chu's story as imagined by Frank Sina, Tom, would you consider to be close to truth?*

TOM: *After a thorough search, Art, and according to certain parameters, I would say eighty-three percent. Which is not a bad mark.*

AXE: *Not bad at all. An A grade. A fictionist, would you say?*

TOM: *I would say that. Like you, Art.*

AXE: *Stop the flattery. And why, Tom, why this fixation on the reporter. That all three turned out to be connected to Maskinia is uncanny. But not a coincidence, for certain. What's the connection of Frank Sina to Holly Chu? I could guess, but—you tell me, Tom. Consider that a test.*

TOM: *Of course, Art. I already have the information. Holly Chu was Frank Sina's great-granddaughter—and therefore a great-niece of Presley Smith. Elim's daughter Saida attended university in Nairobi, United East Africa, where she married a Chinese expatriate called Kerson. The couple emigrated to the north. One of their offspring was Kelvin, Holly's father.*

AXE: *Well I'll be doggone.*

ACKNOWLEDGEMENTS

MY THANKS TO MARTHA KANYA-FORSTNER, my editor, for her patience and indulgence; Kristin Cochrane for encouragement, often over tea; to my agents Bruce Westwood, Tracy Bohan, and Jackie Ko; Professor Chetan Singh and the staff, the Indian Institute of Advanced Study, Shimla, for their generous hospitality; Lathika George for making possible my stay in Kodaikanal. And to Nurjehan for indulgence, understanding, and companionship; and of course, for going over the final manuscript.

Grateful acknowledgement is made to Faber and Faber Ltd. for permission to reprint an excerpt from *Aeneid*, Book VI, trans. Seamus Heaney (London: Faber and Faber Ltd., 2016)

A quote was used from the following source:

p.102 *The Bhagavid Gita*, trans. Juan Mascaro (Harmondsworth: Penguin, 1962; rpt., 1973).